GENERAL JACK

AND

THE BATTLE

OF

THE FIVE KINGDOMS

GENERAL JACK AND THE BATTLE OF THE FIVE KINGDOMS

DAVID BUSH

DEDICATION

I dedicate this book to my five year old great nephew
Jack Zarb Adami. He is the inspiration behind the book because of his love of nature. His penchant for conjuring up battle themes with his toy soldiers gave me the idea for the novel.

WHAT THEY SAY ABOUT THE BOOK

On the surface, the novel seems like an exciting adventure story about the friendship between a young boy and a timid tabby cat, but the plot is multi-layered and has so many life lessons entwined throughout. The build-up to the battle scenes was amazing and filled with brilliant tension, especially when General Jack and King Roar come face to face. The friendship between Jack and Miaow was one of the finest relationships I have read in a long time and there are some quite heartbreaking scenes between them. The plot encompasses not only life lessons but also political and social topics too. The storyline reminded me a lot of *Animal Farm*. The author has created a most wonderful story with strong and realistic characters that you genuinely care about. The ending is spectacular and reminds us that life goes on and why it is important to leave your mark for future generations. ***Readers' Favorite***

General Jack is a book young readers will not only pick up, it's also one they'll not put down until the end. It hits all the high points. Intriguing and engaging characters; heroes to root for; fascinating settings; multiple inspiring themes; and images throughout that capture the action taking place on the pages. The novel is an imaginative and innovative story, jam-packed with all of the elements that engage young people to sit down, open a book and disappear into a world of make-believe. ***Hollywood Book Reviews***

The novel is filled with battles, struggles, wry humour, and sly observations of social and political strife. The narration of events provides an intriguing fictional documentary of the clash between right and wrong, good and evil, and animal and human forces that will keep all ages riveted and thoroughly immersed. The blend of battle themes and nature is very nicely balanced and well-done, enhanced by black and white drawings that are detailed and attractive throughout. Readers who seek a blend of epic fantasy, animal-oriented political commentary à la *Watership Down* or *Animal Farm*, and a vivid story of courage and confrontation will find this novel an outstanding tale. It weaves personal and political purpose with a deft, compelling voice designed to keep readers thoroughly engaged to the end. ***Donovan's Literary Services/ Midwest Book Review***

This short adventure novel is an ideal entry point for young fantasy lovers…Brimming with creativity, boasting vivid world-building, and tipping its cap to other classic fantasy authors, Miaow and young General

Jack make a spectacular team in this heartfelt, well-penned tale. *Self-Publishing Review*

The author creates a tale reminiscent of *The Hobbit* or *The Chronicles of Narnia*. Written much like mythology, the author uses five kingdoms of animals to explain occurrences... It is an intriguing tale with a well-rounded protagonist who, though flawed, overcomes his shortcomings to reach his full potential. The follow-up study guide offers a variety of thought-provoking, thematic questions to encourage discussion... *The US Review of Books*

It resembles, to a considerable degree, children's fictional works by acclaimed past authors J. R. R. Tolkien and C. S. Lewis. I loved reading this book because of its powerful and highly imaginative plot. In it, I found the line on the Reedsy website "There'd be treasure buried here" come amazingly true. *Reedsy Discovery*

A cleverly plotted story reminiscent of George Orwell's *Animal Farm* and populated with an array of interesting, often even charismatic, animal characters. *Wishing Shelf*

An engaging and imaginative but grisly tale that includes a section of paragraphs to help readers understand similar moments in history. Well-formulated scenes with descriptive characters help bring this strategic felines-at-war narrative to life. *Indie Reader Discovery*

I enjoyed reading this riveting novel that follows an ordinary character who does something that he had believed impossible. The plot of the story was intriguing and unique. I also enjoyed the thrilling conflict at the heart of this story. The author has created a unique story that blends *The Jungle Book* with *The Lord of the Rings* to create an enchanting adventure. The book is a spellbinding story that will appeal to fans of epic fantasy. *Literary Titan*

A dense but absorbing adventure packed with overt literary references and layers of meaning. *Kirkus Review*

From the very first page, I was captivated. I found this book to be very entertaining and humorous. I didn't want the story to end. It's been a while that I read a book as hilarious and exceptional as this book. The characters were well-developed. Some scenes are described with such clarity and accuracy that every creak and sound could be discerned by the reader. The moral lessons to be learned from this book are numerous. ***Online BookClub***

This book is an interesting anthropomorphic adventure which reminded me a lot of *The Chronicles of Narnia* and *The Lion King*. Like *The Chronicles of Narnia*, I could see that the plot of General Jack shares connections to stories in The Bible, although this book could be an entertaining read for any young fantasy fan. ***Love Reading Review***

Bush crafts an immersive, often dark, and highly detailed story of warring animal kingdoms that unfolds in a distinct fantasy realm. With hints of parable, the work offers numerous layers of depth and complexity in addition to reading as pure fantasy. The worldbuilding is unique, thorough, and dynamic, with precise exploration of the history, rules, and structure governing the society at-hand. The novel's prose is clear, satisfying, and written in a bold storytelling voice reminiscent of classic works of children's literature. The action, dialogue, and conflict effectively enliven the storytelling. The fine graphics also provide welcome visual texture. ***The BookLife Prize.***

General Jack and the Battle of the Five Kingdoms is a story of adventure, espionage, and learning to nurture self-confidence in the face of adversity. Readers will love the dynamic characters, deep-seated and relevant themes, and adventurous spirit of this book. ***The Book Review Directory.***

All the complete book reviews can be accessed on my Goodreads blog. https://www.goodreads.com/author/show/20529382.David_Bush/blog

FOREWORD

This short novel is an anthropomorphic saga spanning three generations of the protagonist's family. It is geared for the young adult reader, but aspects of it may also appeal to older adults, or rather to the child within adults of all ages.

The book is intended to be entertaining, thought-provoking and educational. For the latter reason, I have included end notes in the back matter. These are extraneous to the story and can be ignored by the casual reader. The back matter is intended as an intimation or invitation only for the turned-on young reader, who may wish to explore topics touched upon in the novel, particularly political history.

For the reader who is interested, there are a dozen or so cross-references in the text to excerpts in the back matter. They draw parallels in the narrative to pivotal real-life historical events. Again, although these excerpts are superfluous to the plot narrative itself, I feel they may impart credibility to the allegorical nature of the story, giving the plot a myth & legend slant.

David Bush
November 2020

ACKNOWLEDGEMENTS

"It's amazing, when you arrive at an impasse in your quest, decisive help arrives out of nowhere. It comes from where you least expect it..." General Jack.

Self-publishing is a lonely affair. With a limited budget, I had to be self-reliant for every aspect of the job. I was the Jack of all trades even though I was a master of none. Of mistakes, I made plenty.

Professional book reviewing is useful but it is costly, commercial and impersonal. A special word of thanks goes out to the sincere, well-meaning Reedsy Discovery reviewer who went beyond his call of duty. He recognised the potential of the ARC, but conceded that much more needed to be done for the book to be a success. He reached out to me privately to suggest ways on how to improve the book. These many suggestions were taken on board and were much appreciated.

A word of thanks goes to an acquaintance of mine blessed with a literary passion, Mary Galea Debono. She enthusiastically volunteered to read the text twice, helping with the editing, proof reading and she provided valuable comments aplenty.

Finally, I appreciate the patience which the graphic designer of Book Cover4u displayed when he strove to accommodate my exigent ideas in the design of the book cover. He continued to help when the book was republished even though our contract had been previously closed.

Not in the clamour of the crowded street,
Not in the shouts and plaudits of the throng,
But in ourselves, are triumph and defeat.

Henry Wadsworth Longfellow

TABLE OF CONTENTS

TABLE OF FIGURES

And God said, "Let the waters bring forth swarms of living creatures, and let birds fly above the earth across the firmament of the heavens." So God created the great sea monsters and every living creature that moves, with which the waters swarm, according to their kinds, and every winged bird according to its kind. And God saw that it was good. **Genesis 1:20-21...**And God said," Let the earth bring forth living creatures according to their kinds: cattle and creeping things and beasts of the earth according to their kinds." And it was so. **Genesis 1:24.**

Then God said, "Let us make man in our image, after our likeness; and let them have dominion over the fish of the sea, and over the birds of the air, and over the cattle, and over all the earth, and over every creeping thing that creeps upon the earth." **Genesis 1:26...** And God saw everything that he had made, and behold, it was very good. And there was evening and there was morning, a sixth day. **Genesis 1:31.**

Author's note

This fable unfolds in the timeless period following the sixth day of creation, in the Garden of Eden just after the birth of Adam and Eve's family.

CHAPTER 1

THE WORLD OF THE FIVE KINGDOMS

he times were dark. They had always been dark and they will remain so. These times had no beginning and they had no end. It was an unpleasant fact of life. It could not be otherwise. That was the way of the world. Self-preservation was paramount. The code of life was to devour and not be devoured. For those of us who could not devour, life was a never-ending run to avoid being devoured. The undulations of the days proceeded with the majestic monotony of sunrise and sundown. The operative word was survival at all costs. Living was a zero-sum game of conquerors and conquered. The only safety for the conquered was to expect no safety. The times were dark indeed

I

My name is Miaow and this is my story. I am the chief of the cats, timid by nature. I am a loyal and obedient subject of the King. I cannot but heed the fierce call of the King and I grovel to stay alive. My name is not difficult to remember, but easy to forget.

King Roar is the terrible, almighty monarch of Our Land. His word is law. With iron fangs and claws, he had slashed his way to the throne. The roar of the throne was his as long as he lived. No other fierce feline had ever managed to out-slash him.

One bleak morning, King Roar summoned me for an assignment. He ordered me to collect sheaves of leaves containing a herbal stimulant which the lions consumed in large quantities. The substance increased their muscle power, sharpened their reflexes and increased their stamina. It was a performance-boosting grass that was grown and harvested in an area controlled by the hyenas. Therein lay the problem because the hyenas were not cooperating. I told the King that.

"You will make them cooperate and deliver it here by noon tomorrow. You are dismissed. Go!" he ordered.

I humbly protested, "But they won't-"

"But they won't nothing," the King thundered. He slashed my face with his sharp claws. Then, he grabbed my tail and swung me forcefully across the room. "You get them or you die. If you escape, we'll slaughter your family."

I hurriedly set off with a heavy heart after an hour or so. There was an air of despondency about the desolate approach to the ridge that led into the valley of the hyenas. No animals were in sight. There was a reason for the absence of non-feline animals; because on the way, I noticed a lion approaching a score of other lions who were seemingly discussing some grave matter. They ignored me, and I descended into the valley. I found myself in the midst of about fifty intimidating hyenas. I relayed King Roar's request.

"We'll do, *what*?" fumed Spotty the leader of the hyenas. "Tell Roar to go to hell. The grass is ours."

"King Roar won't permit it." I said with contrived authority.

"As for you, my dear boy, you've just stepped into hell. You've no way out." Spotty quipped menacingly. The hyenas swarmed around me. I was trapped. There was no way I could escape. There were too many of them. "That's what you get for ordering us about, you worthless feline," and he smashed his clenched paw into my face.

"I-I-If you do anything to me, King Roar will come in person to punish you. He wants his grass by tomorrow and he shall get it."

"Try pulling the other leg, sonny," and Spotty threw me into the crowd of cheering hyenas. "That's *not* the way of the King. He never comes in person. He sends his platoons. Where are they? Do you see any platoons, boys?"

The mob of hyenas was whipped into a frenzy. They joined in the sport. I was mocked, jostled, pushed around, humiliated, but at least, I was alive.

Spotty raised his arms to quell the crowd. "I'll tell you what, boys. Why don't we play Russian roulette with this whiskered slug?" He slowly approached me and pushed his ugly face into my petrified face. "I'll ask you twelve riddles. If you get the questions right, I'll pull out one of your whiskers. If you get it wrong, I'll go for your jugular and drink the blood out of you. The rest of the boys here, will help themselves to the rest of you. What do you say, boys?" he shouted to his cheering companions for approval.

"Bang the drums, boys! Let the game commence…"

"One. What arrow is brown with a green tip?" he asked, as he lifted me off the ground and pressed me against a brown tree trunk. Spotty delivered an uppercut. During the recoil, I caught a glimpse of the green foliage above. "A tree! A tree!" I screamed.

"There's one whisker gone, boys." I cried with pain as he held up the loose whisker for his laughing companions who applauded loudly.

"Two." He grabbed me and spread me on the ground. The sun was in my eyes. I was blinded, "What is the hot ball that goes up and down?" Spotty asked the second riddle.

"The sun! The sun!" I shouted desperately. There went another whisker but I was still alive.

"Three," The jeering hyenas shouted in unison. "Which animal has two tails?" was the third riddle.

"An elephant, one in front, one behind," was my agonizing answer. I lost my third whisker to wild cheering.

"Four. Which animal has the most hairy face?" Spotty snarled.

"A lion! A lion!" I answered. I lost my fourth whisker.

Furious at being outsmarted, Spotty threw me face first into the ground. My face was smashed into the sand. In his frustration, he roughly overturned a broken tree trunk over me. My head was forcibly buried in the sand and I struggled to breathe.

"Five." Spotty sneered, "What is round and-"

Suddenly, the laughter and cheers stopped. There was silence. Spotty's grip lightened. He released his paws. I heard the protracted sound of shuffling feet. Then, there was eerie silence. I lay in that position for about half an hour as I struggled to free myself from the tree trunk. Once freed, I wiped the sand out of my eyes and off my face. I spat out the dust as I looked around. There was no one. The valley was deserted. In the distance,

I noticed a heap of sheaves. I quickly loaded them onto the cart and retraced my steps to the seat of the Feline Kingdom. But I could not understand why I was let off so lightly.

I made the delivery to the King in person. He stared at me contemptuously. "You look *grotesque*! Where *are* your whiskers?" He yelled. "How dare you insult me?"

He threw me across the floor and kicked me out of the room. "A cat without whiskers is no feline. You *are* a disgrace to the feline world. Don't you ever show yourself in my presence until your whiskers grow."

I tottered out, tail between my legs. I carried myself, bruised ego and all, home. As I licked my wounds, I pored over the events of the day. I could not make heads or tails of the episode, but at least, I was still living my first life. I was consoled by the fact that I had not yet used up my eight spare lives. Possibly, I had many more. The other cats reckoned I was the cat of a hundred lives.

Why had the hyenas given in so unexpectedly? I concluded I was born under a lucky star. That, in short, was the story of my life.

I was intimated of what really happened a year later by a sparrow, who had had a birds' eye view of the episode. The lions on the ridge had come together and moved to the edge of the valley. They needed to get a better view of the distant grounds where they were planning a hunting expedition. The lions ignored the happenings in the hyena valley. Frankly, they were not interested. They could not care less. Nevertheless, as soon as the hyenas caught sight of the lions, the vile canines sullenly scurried off without a word into the woods. They left the precious grass behind. The hyenas must have thought that I was not bluffing after all, when I had spoken about King Roar's threatened retribution if the merchandise was not delivered.

Many years ago in animal time, all the animals of the world lived in one large land mass.**(Page179,#1)** Only the western part of the land mass was inhabited. It was called Our Land. This land was bright, green and chirpy. It was a beautiful land. There were plains, hills, valleys, colourful flowers and fruit, wooded areas... Our Land had it all! There were even the ice cold, shimmering, blue lakes and the icy stepping stones bridging the gushing rivers. The larger eastern part of the

land mass beyond the mountains was known as the Dark Land. No one knew what lurked there. The border between Our Land and the Dark Land was composed of two parts. In the northern part, there was the

dividing mountain range. The southern part of the range merged into an immense yellow, parched and inhospitable wasteland that repelled everyone. No one had ever ventured beyond the entire eastern divide. Our Land was hemmed in at the north, west and south borders by a never

ending Great White Ice Lake. No one could ever travel in this infinite white land.

Our habitat was to change in a way no one expected following the coming of a boy from another world.

III

There were five animal kingdoms, but one kingdom ruled them all. King Roar the lion was the omnipotent monarch of the Feline Kingdom. Everything proceeded from him and everything returned to him. The fearsome felines backed the king. They prowled throughout the land. King Roar was the centre of the circle of life and the fierce felines set the law. They conditioned the way of life of all other animals. These felines were born to kill. That was their oxygen. They killed not only for nourishment.

9

It went beyond that. They killed for the sake of killing. It was their *raison d'être*. Their blood sports were particularly cruel but they derived considerable entertainment from these life games. For us animal subjects, life was distilled into a sombre matter of life and death, of good and evil.

All five kingdoms were stratified in a similar manner. A leader, in effect a virtual sub-monarch, headed each of the other four disenfranchised kingdoms. Within each kingdom, there was a ruling class and a larger, heterogeneous underclass. Some kingdoms also had a middle class. The underclass was held in thraldom not only by the relatively benevolent upper class of their respective kingdom but also by the dreaded Feline Overlords. The underclass performed menial tasks. Their stewardship of the land was under the despotic rule of their Feline Overlords to whom all proceeds of the land belonged. This Feline Kingdom ruled over the other kingdoms with an iron paw. The circle of life was held together tautly in this irrevocable manner.

All five kingdoms lorded it over the other orphan and tamer animals who in some cases, were not organised enough to form guilds. These were a pathetic lot. They included the sheep, the goats, the cows, the pigs, the chickens, the rabbits and many others. These formed the large base of the animal pyramid on which all other animals preyed. Their reproductive rate was phenomenal even though their life expectancy was so short. They were incapable of one thing - a natural death. On the contrary, they always met violent, bloody ends. All other animals in the four dispossessed kingdoms had developed their survival skills. These wretched, harmless animals on the other hand, had no self-defence mechanisms. They were especially vulnerable.

One day, King Roar ordered me to clean his office. During this chore, I uncovered a vellum document entitled "The Constitution of Our Land." It read:

"The upper-class members in the Kingdom of Felines are the lions and tigers. The king shall always be a lion. He is elected after a contest to the death with any contenders. The survivor is elected King for life or until anyone successfully challenges him. The middle class consists of the

jaguars, the cheetahs, the leopards, the panthers, the cougars and their black cousins - the pumas. The servile cats constitute the underclass.

"The upper class in the Canine Kingdom includes the grey wolves and their cousins. The middle class encompasses the foxes, the coyotes, the jackals, and the hyenas. Then there are those insufferably noisy underdogs.

"The bulls, the buffalos and the bison represent the upper class in the Dairy Kingdom. The stupid cows and cattle form the underclass.

"In the Equine Kingdom, zebras and giraffes are the fancy upper class animals. The deformed camels, gazelles, deer, and elks are the middle class members. The filthy horses, mules and donkeys complete the underclass.

"In the Kingdom of Big Mammals, the clumsy elephants are the masters. The rhinos and overweight hippopotamuses are the middle class while those odious bears constitute the underclass."

This was the hierarchical structure of animal society in those times. It had been like that since time immemorial and it could never change.

But, that social arrangement was about to be shattered forever.

IV

 I was, and still am, an accident of nature. Believe it or not, I had been reluctantly roped in and elected chief of the cats. Even my election was shrouded in controversy. The losing candidate did not concede graciously. He alleged a selection bias in my favour, as the cats had overlooked the fact that I was afraid of my own shadow. Fate intervened though. It so happened that our convention was rudely interrupted by a stampeding cattle herd. My challenger was amongst those who were trampled to death while I escaped unscathed. The call of nature had had its say and the election was thus decided. I always thought that fate behaved in mysterious ways whenever I was concerned.

Us cats, we are the most numerous but the most disadvantaged of the dwellers in the land. Our masters treat us badly, though they do not consider us capable of being anything but loyal to them. We are their black sheep blood relations. They tolerate us because they need us. We throw ourselves at their mercy in order to survive. On the other hand, no animals trust us because of our close relations to the Overlords. In fact, they detest us because in other animals' eyes, we are diminutive replicas of their Overlords. Moreover, they regard us as spies or accomplices of the detested Lords of the Land. For them, we are *animale non grata*. Everyone holds us in contempt. We are doubly cursed.

This attitude on the part of other fellow animals was about to change following the advent of our friend, Jack.

Until then, I had always lived in fear. I developed good survival skills. I trained my eyes, ears and nose to see, hear and smell danger long before it could materialise. Mine was a suspicious, non-trusting mind. Danger lurked everywhere. I imagined it, even when it was not there and the heightened awareness served me well. This complex kept me alive. I was a fast runner; I was a good climber of trees. Besides, I had sharp reflexes. Longevity was the reason for my election as chief of the cats. I was the insignificant chief of an insignificant race in Our Land.

That was the recurring theme of my life. A friendly, unseen hand was always reaching out to help me, but I was forever running away from it. Opportunity scared me. I shuddered to think of the consequences if one day, I were unable to run from this invisible hand. With my running days over, I would be all but dead.

I had seen so many animals being sadistically devoured. I became desensitised like everyone else, until it affected my immediate family. Losing the two sisters I had grown up with, had traumatised me. They were the victims of the feline masters' hateful game, the "Cat Run". King Roar organised a tournament between the different fierce feline factions where three cats were released into a closed, depressed, huge arena from which there was no escape. These games were presided by King Roar who saw off the three running victims. The feline contestants relentlessly hunted them down. The two feline teams competed in amassing their grisly trophies, scoring points according to the body part, the colour of the body part and the speed with which they earned their trophies. The team that accumulated the most points won.

The loss of my dear wife traumatised me as well. A savage group of marauding coyotes had cut her down. I was frightened and I scampered off to safety, abandoning my young family to a cruel fate. My wife struggled to shield our four newly born babies from them. I did nothing. I watched with tear-filled eyes from a safe distance. Oh yes, something I did do! I averted my gaze in shame, when she screamed my name as she desperately cried for help. I walked away before the bloody act was completed. It turned out I had used my family as bait for the predators, so I could escape. I owe my life to the self-sacrifice of my wife.

I had also lost my parents to the fury of the wolves. The wolves hated the felines, but they vented all their hatred on the weakest of the felines, us. They did not dare touch the feline masters. We regularly had to venture into the territories of the four defunct kingdoms on official business for our masters. These were hazardous journeys. Our masters made no effort to protect or defend us. My parents died on one of these tax-collecting missions in black wolf territory. I remember the day clearly because it was my first birthday; so I was excited. My mother had a sinister premonition that day. She insisted on going with Dad to protect him in any which way she could. She explained that two cats stood a better chance of survival than one alone! They pledged they would return in time for my birthday party to give me a glorious birthday present. They never returned. I was sad (I wanted my present). I waited for days on end, but they never came and I never received my birthday present. To this day, I do not know where their remains are. I can only imagine the ordeal they went through in the final hour of their lives.

V

My whiskers had not yet grown. The collecting missions had to be done, though I still could not present myself to the King, so I recruited the help of my two sons, Purr and Scratchy.

One day, while on such a mission, I was walking with my two sons. On the way, Scratchy was his usual playful, happy-go-lucky self. There was a large group of grazing zebras. He could not resist the urge to tease them, so he departed from our path for some time. When he returned, he pointed out a nearby hollow tree trunk. He said it was the perfect hiding place when he played hide-and-seek with his friends. On the under surface, there was a large hole from which a meerkat must have burrowed an underground escape tunnel into the nearby woods. It was an ideal passage for emerging from the tree trunk, thereby victoriously outflanking his opponents. No one else knew of this secret passage.

Purr, a grey tabby cat, remained silent throughout the walk. He was a good listener but he was an animal of few words. It could be because he had such a bad stutter. The demise of his mother had traumatised him. He used to adore her. At such a tender age, he had been completely dependent on her. Deprived of maternal affection, he never regained his confidence. Scratchy, on the other hand, was too young to remember his mother at the time of her passing.

Our mission was completed and we were walking home together. Loud screaming caught our attention. Instinctively, the three of us made our way to the top of the ridge. Below, we beheld a distressing scene, which made me break into a cold sweat. It was a re-enactment of a previous traumatic scene I had witnessed. There were two cats desperately trying to protect their children from a group of marauding wolves.

It was a disturbing *déjà vue* sight and I quickly told my sons, "Come on, let's go home. There's nothing we can do here. It doesn't concern us."

I turned to move on, but my feet remained stuck to the ground. My glassy, tremulous eyes were still focused on the scene, even though my body was turned in the opposite homeward direction. I could not turn away. Something was holding me back. I stared at the face of the mother cat. It reminded me of my wife's face. From a distance, she seemed to look back at me. Our eyes met for an instant. The expression on her face said, "*Will you turn away again, this time?*" It was the voice of my wife. I suppressed a sob, but I remained as still as a statue.

Purr had already moved a few steps in a homeward direction, but he stopped. He stared back at me when he realised that I did not lead the way home. Scratchy, on the other hand, did not move. For once, he was serious. His gaze flitted from the scene back on to me. It rested on me for some time. He glanced away from me quickly in two different directions. He then looked behind. Swiftly, he departed from my side. The next instant, I became aware of Scratchy charging down the hill holding onto an elephant's thigh bone. I never saw a black cat run so fast. He slammed into the dozen or so wolves. He knocked one over and the others fell over like dominoes. He bowled them all over with one swipe. Scratchy discarded the bone and darted over the plain where he disappeared into his hide-and-seek tree trunk. After the wolves realised what had hit them, they promptly gave chase. I saw them hovering hungrily around the trunk, but Scratchy was safe. After a few minutes, they gave up their search, but in the distance, they must have noticed something which tickled their imagination. The wolves immediately dashed off barking and were not seen again. They were probably chasing the grazing zebras we had seen before.

I ran down the hill. Only two cats survived the massacre. The mother was mortally injured. Her young daughter, a ginger coloured kitten, was badly shaken, but she was untouched. Purr caught up with me and he stared stupidly at the girl.

Purr took care of the funeral arrangements, while I tended the injured cat. I did what I could but it was next to nothing. In fact, it did not amount to anything at all. Or, did it? Life is full of strange surprises and opportunities. That day turned out to be a particularly eventful day.

At nightfall, we all sat by a fire. I took in the silent scene. The girl did not take her admiring eyes off Scratchy who by then, had casually re-joined us. Scratchy's restless eyes danced everywhere but not on any one of us. Undoubtedly, he was thinking of what new adventures the next day would bring. Life for him was one great adventure. Purr did not take his eyes off the girl. The mother's tear-filled gaze was fixed affectionately on

15

her daughter. Every now and then, she shifted her eyes on to me, when I was not looking. She seemed to be sizing me up.

The others were asleep. The mother beckoned me. I moved over to her side.

"Thank you for saving us."

"Err! It wasn't I. It was my son, Scratchy who saved you. I wished to save you, but I couldn't get down to it. My courage failed me. It always does."

"No, *you* saved us. I saw you give the order to your son."

"You're wrong. The only order I gave was to move on. It was none of our business. There was nothing to be done. I did not want to endanger my family and myself. That is the way of the world. As you know, there's no place for heroes in Our Land. There's no honour in heroics. Long live the cowards! The future is theirs." *Future? What am I saying? What future? There is no future.* There were other jarring thoughts but it's best I say no more.

"No, *you* saved us," she reiterated, never taking her unblinking bleary eyes off me. I silently shook my head in denial.

Then she said strange words, "You are heading for a *great* destiny." I uttered a self-depreciatory laugh.

She turned her gaze towards the sleeping daughter. Tears streamed down her face. The mother cat was in poor condition. It was obvious she would not survive long. I looked at her daughter, but my mind's eye saw the newborn babies I had lost in similar circumstances. I was presented with the perfect opportunity to atone for the act of omission in my wife's death. I was hesitant. I was indecisive about the commitment that deep down, I desired.

For the last time, the moribund mother reached out for the sleeping daughter, but her severed arm fell short. Her lips moved but no words came out, only tears. The dramatic scene struck a chord in my heart. She slowly turned her face towards me. I looked down at her but I saw the pleading face of my wife. I shut my eyes and vigorously shook my head to dispel the vision from my mind. I could not take it anymore. It was painful - my heart strings were too taut. There was loud banging on my door inside. Was it my wife knocking? Something gave inside. I had to open up.

"Look, *don't* worry about your daughter," I reassured her eagerly.

She showed no reaction.

The knocking inside was louder. "I promise you, I will look after her," I gushed. "She *will* be safe with me."

She still showed no reaction.

The intrusive knocking was even louder. "I'm renowned for my survival skills. She will be one of the family, I *promise* you," I asserted.

Her expressionless gaze remained fixed on me. She did not bat an eyelid throughout the conversation.

I paused and wondered about her facial expression for a moment. Next, I shook her clumsily, "Are you still alive?" I asked awkwardly. She winced with pain.

"Oh! I'm sorry. I-I-I thought-" my voice trailed off.

Then she said some other strange words, "It is *you* who will need looking after."

"What is your daughter's name?"

"Sabine." She sighed and she fell into a deep slumber. Only then did the persistent knocking stop.

I returned to my place and thought hard. I had always felt bad about my behaviour at the time of my wife's death. I could never shake it off. It was a festering wound. I constantly brooded over it. Somehow, after these latest events, the perpetual heartache I had always felt within, eased. Brusquely, I crawled over silently to Scratchy. I shook him. He sleepily awoke, eyes still closed.

I whispered a question, "Scratchy, *why* did you rescue the family?"

"Because you told me to," he yawned.

"I did nothing of the sort."

"Oh yes you did," he mumbled indifferently.

"I did *not*."

"Yes you did. Your body language pleaded with me to do so."

I was stupefied and speechless for a moment, but then I understood.

"Thank you, son! Thank you!" I blurted out, "If only you know how happy you've made me. I'm so grateful. I'm in your debt, *forever*. What can I do for you, son?" I was effusive in my gratitude, but Scratchy was not listening. He had long fallen asleep. I could not sleep that night. There was a warm glow around me.

In the following days, Scratchy had no recollection of the conversation. I brought it up with him, but he was dismissive. He merely shrugged his shoulders nonchalantly. "I must have been talking in my sleep," he said, "I didn't know what I was saying." Conversely, that eventful night's conversation remained imprinted in my memory. I treasured it all my life, even though Scratchy could not understand what the fuss was all about.

How could a humbug like me produce such a bright spark as Scratchy? Both he and Purr had seen me in that confused state. Purr merely looked at me, but Scratchy looked into me. He had recognised the disconnect between my verbal talk and my heart talk. He saw they were at odds. He was gifted with an incredible sense of discernment. He saw deep into my soul like no other. He not only obeyed my heart talk, but brought it to fruition in a spectacular way. In the nick of time, he had planned and executed the entire rescue operation. He did what I did not do, he did not do what I did.

At dawn, everyone, but the mother, woke up. She had died peacefully in the night. Scratchy had already left us as soon as he awoke. He was the first to wake up and he departed on another of his adventures. Sabine was distraught. Purr stood by respectfully while I clumsily tried to console her. Strangely, while in that afflicted state, Sabine asked after Scratchy. As usual, Purr took care of the funeral arrangements. He handled every detail with his customary delicacy.

I still could not get the incident out of my mind. A few weeks later I brought up the subject with Scratchy yet again. I wondered aloud how he would have reacted had the circumstances been different.

"Why? If you had forbidden it, I wouldn't have intervened."

"What if you had been alone when you witnessed the lynching of Sabine's family?"

"Oh! I'd have definitively intervened." He punched the air triumphantly as he exclaimed, "Yes!"

"Why?"

"For the sheer joy of it. Nothing excites me more than rubbing those big, bad wolves up their backsides."

For me, it was a matter of life and death. For Scratchy, it was all a game.

VI

 The family took to Sabine. She flourished under our care. Scratchy and Sabine were kindred spirits; they had the same passions and desires. They went off on adventures together. They raised hell. Scratchy used to say, "If I can't move the heavens, then I will raise hell." The dynamic duo climbed trees, they chased the birds, they teased the domesticated animals, and they created stampedes. They flew together. They were adept at concluding their missions successfully. They hoodwinked the unsuspecting animals with their cock-and-bull stories. They twisted the arms of the King's subjects to obtain what they requested. The pair of them always got what they wanted out of the dull animals. They both used to return, all laughs and smiles, as they related their wild exploits. These were ingenious, like when they tried to wrest concessions from the troublesome hyenas. The two of them whipped up a stampede of buffalos which overran the hyena grounds. The hyenas never gave us any more trouble thereafter. They finally submitted.

Or, when they whipped up four simultaneous stampedes - the zebras from the north, the mustangs from the south, the antelopes from the west and the giraffes from the east. These all converged on to the central territory of the murderous wolves. After the fracas, Scratchy happily declared to us all, "Sabine's massacred family has finally been avenged," as he briskly rubbed his paws together with gusto. Sabine tiptoed to impishly plant a kiss on the right cheek of his beaming face.

Scratchy had mastered the art of flying. He was a phenomenal high and long jumper. He was a masterful athlete with an incredible spring in his legs. He would nose dive to the ground from one tree top and then bounce up onto the next one, and so on. He brought the ostriches to heel in that manner. The ostriches ran away from threats on the ground. It was impossible to reason with them, they were so elusive. They also evaded separate threats from the air. But they could not handle combined simultaneous threats from both the ground and the air, in the shape of high flying Scratchy. How did they respond? By staying still and burying their heads in the only medium they thought they were safe – *below* the ground.

They were then at our mercy, we could gain any concessions the Feline Masters required of them.

Scratchy was his own master. He enjoyed Sabine's company but he did not need her. He had bags of energy and, at times, she slowed him down. Also, her exuberance and chattiness sometimes interfered with his concentration. He was a cat of action and when in action mode, he was a cat of few words, such was his intensity of purpose. He started to go off more and more on his own. He was always in search of new experiences. Sabine, on the other hand, could not live without Scratchy. She rued the times he would go off and not return for weeks.

Once, I joined her as she was on the hill looking out for Scratchy. She was silently sobbing. I tried to console her.

"Scratchy's like that. He is so gifted, he's self-sufficient. He'll always be a loner. He doesn't need anyone."

"But he doesn't tell me when he's going anymore. He just disappears. It's not fair. I've been so patient with him. I do whatever he says. He has *no* reason to complain about me."

"Sabine, dear… Enjoy him while he's here. We all do. Don't grieve when he's not. He won't ever change. You'll never get the constant security and comfort you crave for, with him. He runs on the wild side of life. He's not a family cat. He's just not cut out for it. He's a cat with the heart of a lion and the humour of a chimpanzee. He'll never lay roots anywhere. He'll keep shooting off at tangents. You should cast your eyes elsewhere. Look at Purr, for instance-"

"*Who?*"

"Purr," I emphasized. "He worships the ground you walk on. He'd walk through hell for you."

"Oh! Purr. *Wait.* Is that Scratchy in the distance? Yes, it is." She squealed with delight and ran off in his direction.

Yes, we all loved Sabine. Twinkle, my eldest fluffy child fussed over her. Purr did his usual mundane chores diligently in between the shy glances he stole at Sabine. He remained in the shadows. They seldom spoke, but his furtive glances said it all. As far as I was concerned, Sabine had a soothing effect on me. Her presence among us went some way in calming that vociferous voice inside, which was always berating me for not doing enough.

 Twinkle posed a serious dilemma for me. There was not a single bad bone in her. She was good-natured through and through. Her problem was that she saw only the good in everyone else. That was the crux of the Twinkle enigma. She was too trusting and she was my worst nightmare. Striving to keep her alive was a headache because she was hopelessly out of place in Our Land. Left to her own means, she would have approached a hyena to clean his slimy, ugly nose. Or, she would have scolded the drooling, angry wolf for soiling the beautiful land with his disgusting spittle.

I went through great lengths to deny her existence. Each head of household had to provide a census to the King about every member of the household, including all the births and the deaths. I kept Twinkle off the census. On paper, she did not exist. She was officially deceased. I ran a big risk. It was a crime punishable by death not only for me, but for all the family. She spent most of her sheltered life in her homestead. She never ventured far from its environs. Her naiveté was such, that if she ever came into contact with a fierce feline, she would do or say something silly that would claim her life. If her name ever appeared on the census, being the only daughter of a known feline chief, her life expectancy would have been a matter of minutes or hours. Once she commented that the King's beard was too big and untidy. It needed to be shaved. Besides, she claimed he was in dire need of a haircut. She said she would go to the King in person and offer to trim his beard. She would not have lasted a minute in his presence.

One day, I was eating the food Twinkle had dutifully prepared for me. Twinkle revealed that she had made a few small wooden containers for the wolves to spit into, rather than having them spit on the ground. She held one up for me to see and proudly called it a spit-box. I nodded vacantly and continued eating. But then she said she was going into wolf territory to gift them personally to the wolves. I doubled up, overturning my dish.

"You will do nothing of the sort," I thundered and I banged my clenched paw on the table. "I forbid it."

Sabine turned round startled by my violent outburst. She gave me an admonishing sidelong look which put me to shame.

She promptly interjected happily, "Oh Twinkle! What a wonderful idea. Leave it to me, I'll distribute them to the wolves for you. It will save you the trouble. It's no trouble for me because it's on my way. You can stay here doing what you enjoy. You've got plenty to do, I see."

I stared hard at Sabine in disbelief. She returned my cold look with a reassuring one. If only, I had her tact! The kitten had come of age under my very eyes and I had not even noticed. All this time, I had been too self-absorbed to notice.

Sabine left, leaving me in the company of Twinkle who sang her usual lullabies, "What a sweet child Sabine is!" "Isn't Sabine the sunshine of our household?" "Where would we be without Sabine?" (up to that point I silently agreed, but then…) "Oh Dad, it was so clever of you to bring Sabine to us," "Dad, tell me about your brainwave that brought Sabine to us?" Twinkle's recital went on and on. I finished my meal as quickly as possible. When I was done and dusted, I took leave of her, announcing in a martial tone "Well Twinkle, thank you. I'd love to stay, but duty calls," and I marched out (thank goodness). As I walked off, I could hear Twinkle humming sugary tunes to herself. No doubt the humming would continue all day until Sabine returned to relight the fire of Twinkle's life.

When I had related Sabine's story to Twinkle, she was moved beyond words. Twinkle wanted to mother Sabine and she tried to smother Sabine with affection. But Sabine would have none of it. Like Scratchy, there was a fierce, independent streak in Sabine, even though she was still a child. In her endearing way Sabine battled with Twinkle. She countered Twinkle's mothering with her own mothering, to great effect. Whenever Twinkle pampered her, Sabine always gave her the slip. She would run off on one of her adventures with Scratchy, but she always made it a point to bring a memento of her adventure for Twinkle. She relished these gifts. They were herbs, plants, flowers, seeds, whatever. Sabine would tell her some ridiculous story of how Twinkle could change them into something magical. And incredibly, my vacuous daughter used to swallow the bait - hook, line and sinker - each time. She would spend her days humming silly songs in praise of Sabine while she crushed the ingredients into her creations. Twinkle produced scents and fragrances, soaps, perfumes, detergents, conditioners and even medicines, she claimed.

I had had enough of this quackery. There was always a strong flowery scent in the house. My eyes began watering. My nose started dripping. I was constantly sneezing. I was not feeling too well and I was having breathing difficulties. Besides, Twinkle's heartfelt lullabies were getting me on my nerves. I could not take it anymore, so I decided to move out. I wanted to build a hut nearby and live alone. All the while, from my new vantage point, I would still be able to keep a protective eye on Twinkle. I had to make sure she did not venture into the dangerous, wild areas. Her safety was always uppermost on my worrying mind.

As I was packing up my possessions, Sabine happened to enter the room. She observed me and she was surprised, "What are you doing? Where are you going with all those things?"

I told her everything. I confided in her and angrily listed all my complaints and ailments. I could not be more pedantic than that.

Sabine was alarmed. She said, "Please don't go. It will destroy Twinkle when she finds out. She'll blame herself for your departure. She dotes on you so much. I'll take care of it. Leave Twinkle to me. I'll talk to her. Only promise me that you'll delay your departure for three days. Scratchy's waiting for me now, but when I return, I'll deal with it."

Three days later, Twinkle came bursting into the room in an agitated state, "Dad, you *have* to move out. It's *not* safe for you here. Please move out, Dad. It's for your *own* good. Don't take it against me. I'll help you build a hut close by. Anything, but move out *today*. I'm so sorry but I don't want to hurt you. I promise I'll come by every day to look after you, to clean your place and to prepare your food."

So, I happily moved out into lodging next door and physically, I felt much better in the subsequent days. I sneezed and wheezed no more.

The next day, I found Sabine alone in Twinkle's house, "Sabine, I'm curious. What cock-and-bull story did you invent this time, for Twinkle to do the impossible and throw me out of *my own* house?"

"Oh! I told Twinkle, that you weren't well with all that sneezing. I told her, all those herbs and pollens were not doing you any good. Your body was reacting and fighting against them. You were the victim of those invisible battles and it was harming you. Your chest was even starting to make funny noises. I told Sabine, that if you stayed a day longer, the battles might become too bad and leave you defeated. You could collapse, lose consciousness, stop breathing and maybe, even die."

"Did you need to be *so* melodramatic, Sabine? You scared poor Twinkle out of her wits!"

Sabine shrugged her shoulders, "But you wanted to move out, didn't you? I didn't want you to hurt Twinkle's feelings. That's all. I knew you'd have regretted hurting her afterwards."

At that instant, Twinkle returned, "Dad," she said glowing with pride, "Your hut's ready. I'm sure you'll like the way I arranged it for you."

I was about to depart with Twinkle, but Sabine called out, "By the way Twinkle, I gave your spit-boxes to the wolves and guess what? They loved them. They told me to convey their thanks to you. They each said they'll carry it with them wherever they go, because they found it very convenient."

"That's wonderful, Sabine. But no, they can't have just one or two spit-boxes. No, I'll make many more for them and you can distribute them in my name."

I rolled my eyes in dismay, threw my arms in the air, and went off alone to my lodgings shaking my head all the way. I left the girls behind merrily talking their flowery small talk.

If only I could be as tactful as Sabine. I just did not have the patience. Sabine had managed to relieve not only my heartache, but even my headache. Also, the nightmares concerning Twinkle's safety became less frequent. I was secure in the knowledge that Twinkle would be safe, thanks to Sabine's craftiness. Twinkle would lead a long, loving and productive life, now that she had discovered her calling to motherhood. She had firmly resolved to take Sabine's dead mother's place. Twinkle spent most of her time at home, cooking, cleaning, experimenting and producing her quackeries. There was no limit to her creativity. All the while, she happily sang ballads in praise of Sabine and the world in general. But her happiest time of the day, was when Sabine returned home with Scratchy. It was a never ending joy for Twinkle to welcome Sabine home each time. One would have thought that each meeting was to be their last ever meeting in Our Land. Twinkle was so passionate, she wore her heart on her paw sleeve.

Sometimes, I wondered who the mother really was! Was it Twinkle or was it Sabine? In my opinion, Sabine had beaten Twinkle at my daughter's own sparring game. For me, Sabine had triumphed in the motherhood battle. Sabine the child was the *de facto* mother. Twinkle my daughter was the *de jure* surrogate mother, though officially of course, Twinkle did not exist.

VIII

 I dreamt many dreams. I found comfort in rhapsodising. There was one particular recurring dream - I had morphed into a lion who mounted a successful challenge to King Roar. As the new king, I set the law of the land. I abolished the blood sports. I repaired relations with the other four kingdoms. Most important of all, I drafted legislation to protect the disenfranchised orphan animals. None of the Kingdoms claimed these animals. I felt for these helpless, wretched souls. I had a visceral understanding of their plight because I had experienced it myself.

One day I had an unusual dream. Was it a dream or was it delirium? Dream or not, I was being carried in two strong paws. I lay bleeding at death's door. The cocoon shell in which I had always sought refuge had been shattered. I was about to embark on a long, arduous journey of self-discovery. How scared I was! My dread of the unknown and the feeling of uncertainty distressed me. The rearward receding glimpse of the broken cocoon filled me with regret. At least, I had been safe there. Now, I was in unfamiliar territory. The future obstacles were menacing. I did not have the attributes to grapple with them. In some way, my fears were eased by the knowledge that I was in safe hands. I will never forget that day, nor the events leading up to that dream.

CHAPTER 2

THE MAKING OF GENERAL JACK

I

will never forget that tumultuous day. It was serene and sunny. The blue sky was cloudless. I was famished as I had not eaten for three days. In a grassy enclosure, a strong scent attracted me. I stumbled across the fresh severed carcass of a big lioness. It must have been involved in a vicious fight and abandoned in a pitiable state. The scene was desolate. No live animal could be seen, smelt or heard in the vicinity. This was a pleasant surprise. My prayers had been answered. Delicious food had fallen into my path from the heavens above. It was too good to be true. No one had claimed the food.

I guzzled my meal with relish. For that reason, my senses were dulled. The strong smell of the food masked a faint scent behind me. The greedy gurgling sounds of my gut drowned out the faint rustle of grass behind me. My eyes feasted on the lavish choice of the glorious meal in front of me. In a flash, a huge black panther struck me down from behind. He pounced before I could react. His fangs dug into me and he flung me around. Escape was futile. Helplessness reigned and everything turned black. The aggressor left me for dead and I lay bleeding there for the entire day. There was one particularly deep mortal gash on the left side of my trunk and flank. I could not move on, as one of my hind legs was broken. There were many other gashes, but the main exsanguinating flank wound was the death of me. I was feverish. I was dying.

Thoughts chased each other feverishly in my fading mind. One of

these was the vision of my epitaph, which read, *"This is Miaow who dreamt big dreams but never achieved anything."* The vultures circled above me in the bleary sky. The scent of the hyenas lurking in the woods permeated from the left. To the right, the heaving breath and the restless pacing of the wolves was within earshot. My last wish was to die intact with dignity. After I gave up my ghost, the predators could fight it out between themselves for my remains as much as they liked.

I made laboured movements from time to time to demonstrate my vitality to the loitering predators. It was the only way in which I could put off the final onslaught I dreaded. With time however, my strength failed me. The predators saw only a still cat in their field of operation. They commenced their tentative approach towards me. They halted when they heard an unremitting whine coming from what they thought was a corpse. There was still life in the beaten cat after all. *Will this cat never die?* The incessant whine became softer and softer until it failed altogether.

My blurred visual fields contracted. The circling black shapes in the blue sky became progressively larger. The scent to the left of me became more acute. The menacing sounds to the right of me were louder. My last wish was not to be granted after all. Even in this, I had failed!

Then I made the single most important act of my entire life. I summoned whatever was left of my strength in desperation. I let out the last searing, ear-piercing cry of my life. A few minutes later, the miracle happened. An apparition approached me from the east. I did not know whether I was dreaming or not. I was delirious. Two strong paws gently hoisted me off the ground. The sudden change in altitude made me black out.

II

I said it was a miracle. I lie! It was not a miracle but a series of miracles in quick succession.

I regained my senses under a still indigo evening sky. My eyes opened. I squinted through the shimmering light and focused on a silhouette. By my side was a boy, lithe in form. His hair was straight and auburn. The fringe on his forehead accentuated his deep blue eyes. His freckled nose was tilted skyward and his face was bronzed. What a pleasing sight it was! That was the first miracle. I had never savoured such a vision in my life. Nor would I see anything remotely like it in the rest of my long life.

He caressed my bloodied peel gently with his strange tapered paws. He inspected and nursed the wound. He patiently fed me. Later, he sprinkled me with water and washed me inside out. The cool, clear water was refreshing. I had been all but dead. These nursing measures however, reinvigorated me. He laid me down in a comfortable bed. I reclined in a secluded grassy space under the foliage of a W-shaped tree. That was the second miracle. Nothing like that had ever happened in the animal world. Everyone to himself - that is the motto of our world. No one cared for anyone else, except of course, the mother for her newborn.

Then, the third miracle. He spoke animal language. His name was Jack. He had descended from the eastern range. Jack wanted to see more of the world. That day he was on the move but, my last dying cry attracted his attention. For some reason I could not then understand, he referred to it as the Call of the Siren. He said he would stay with me for a few more weeks until I was better. Then he would resume his travels.

The fourth miracle. Jack slowly but surely, nursed me back to full health. How that happened was beyond me. Those convalescent weeks were the happiest time of my life. Jack resuscitated me not only physically but also psychologically. Within me, he planted an unknown seed. I had no idea what it was. All I knew - I was dead, but now I was alive. I had been reborn.

One time I was asleep. I woke up and looked around. Jack was sitting a few yards away from me, with his back to me. He thought I was asleep but he softly sang a lullaby to himself:

"In the land of caverns
A master ran the tavern
A hungry dog did feed at table
All partook they of the fable

When the day was done
All did depart but one
The master did he then journey far
The dog with love did watch the master's star

The years went by
The master did not he pass by
The dog hungry it waited for the image
The dog with joy it yelped at the mirage

The day had come, the dog was numb
The master he had come
The dog with joy was overcome
Thus so the dog did it succumb"

During those convalescent days, we chatted and became friends. He was keen to know more about our way of life. His age was fourteen. Those fourteen years endowed him with wisdom beyond his age. He asked a multitude of probing questions.

I explained to him that all the animals were too weak, divided or indifferent to mount a challenge to Feline Rule. Although the ruling kingdom was in a minority, their grip on power was uncontested. The Feline Masters and the various animal clans had clashed in many small-scale skirmishes throughout the ages. The felines brutally suppressed the revolts. The Feline Kingdom was invincible. Any resistance was futile.

During those conversations, I bared my soul. I gave vent to my fears, frustrations and shortcomings. My emotions and passions burst forth like cascading water through a broken dam. Fate had split me open. My character and personality were exposed. Disillusioned, I shied away from the dark reflection of my inner self. I did not like what I saw. Jack was interested and patient. He calmly listened to my repetitive lamentations.

"What do you wish for most of all?" he asked.

"Why! To overthrow King Roar and the Feline Kingdom of course." Then I told him about my recurring dream.

"But that's just escapism. Nothing can come out of it. You're deluding yourself. You're merely trying to escape reality. A cat you are and a cat you will remain. You cannot pretend to be what you are not. Fantasizing makes you feel better during the dream, but it makes matters worse in the wider scope of life. Afterwards, it increases your frustration and sense of futility. Those two feelings fester inside and consume you."

"It's not just the frustrations that are eating me up. It's the anger as well."

"What anger?" Jack asked, "Is it anger with the felines?"

"No. Not with the felines. They are what they are. The blood of cruel killers flows in their veins. They can't help it. They can't change. It's more anger with the animals of the four dysfunctional kingdoms. Some of them have the strength and attributes to challenge the felines but they don't care. Each one only thinks about himself at the expense of everything else. It's also anger with myself. I should do something, but I don't do whatever it is I have to do. There is also indignant anger about the plight of the other cats and especially of the countless orphan animals."

"Well Miaow, at least that is something. Everyone else is self-centred. You're not like that. It seems there is something special in you, after all."

"We both know I'm useless".

"If you want something, you go for it. Don't you?"

I nodded.

"So, if you want to overthrow the felines, overthrow them!"

"That can never happen. I know it. Everyone knows it."

"Well, never say never."

"It's impossible!"

"Well… Concentrate on the possible in the word impossible. It's easy. You just have to ignore the first two letters of the word and the impossible becomes possible."

"It can never happen. It has always been so and it will remain so forever."

"Well… There has to be a new beginning. Everything has to have a beginning and an end. You cannot have one without the other. It applies to everything, even Feline Rule for that matter. It began at some point in time and it will come to an end."

"But they are too strong. They are a superpower."

"Well…Every institution, no matter how powerful, has its weaknesses. Anything that rises has to fall. But why are the felines so invincible?"

"They have it all - the cruelty, the malice, the strength, the majesty and the ability to dominate all life."

"But you said that the aristocrats of the other kingdoms match them in these qualities. The bears have the cruelty but not the other traits. The wolves have the malice but not the other traits. The elephants have the strength but not the other traits. The giraffes have the majesty but not the other traits. What if they were to coalesce into one unit? That would satisfy their individual hankering for self-preservation. Together, they'd merge into one "hybrid feline figure" that outsmarts the actual feline. This hybrid can then dominate life."

"It sounds well in theory but in practice it can never happen."

"Why not? You need three conditions for that to happen. You already have the first and most important one. The other two flow from the one you already have. You already have a shared objective, right? You can't deny that every single animal hates Feline Rule and wants it to be overthrown."

"What are the other two?"

"They are the *esprit de corps* and the sense of mission."

"Oh! That can never happen! Forget it! Animals were created that way. There is no sense of camaraderie between them. They may stick together but they do not stick up for each other. The *esprit de corps* does not apply within their own blood race, let alone for the animals of the other races."

"That's where you come in."

"*What*? You're crazy! What difference can I make?"

Jack rose impatiently. Then, he said as his gesticulations enhanced the tone of his voice, "I *have* already told you. You *are* special. You are unique in that you care. You already have that sense of comradeship that everyone else lacks. Only you can impart it to the others."

"But they all hate us for being felines."

"That's exactly it," he re-joined, "that is why you will succeed. That hatred will ironically be your strength and weapon. You and your cats are united. You occupy a strategic position in society, as you are the link between the Feline Kingdom, the other four kingdoms and the orphans. What will the non-felines make of your covert defection from the felines? The non-felines do not fear the cats. You are no threat to them. You have everything to lose, you in particular, as the chief. Everyone will know it. If uncovered, the cats will suffer a terrible fate. Nobody will be spared. That's how felines deal with treachery, particularly treachery from within their ranks. The non-felines will wonder as to the underlying motive of your defection. They will come around to the realisation of the cats' courage and principled stand. Your efforts will win the respect, admiration and trust of the other animals in a measure equal to the hatred they now have for you. The stance on the part of the cats would be unprecedented. It won't pass unnoticed. 'Why?' the animals would ask themselves, 'are the cats doing this?' The answer would be obvious. 'They are doing it not only for themselves but also for a common good, for a higher ideal from which every non-feline benefits. They do it for others at a great personal cost.' They know that the cost you will incur if things go pear shaped is much higher than their own price. So you see, in your small way, the cats' influence will be disproportionately high in the non-feline world."

"But what about the sense of mission?"

"Well. You must have a doable roadmap. You have to be patient, and discreet. One measure will lead to another. You need to have solid, inspiring leadership, someone who devises clinical strategies and plans. I'm sure there is someone from the non-feline ranks who fits the bill and-"

"I'm not sure about that," I interrupted. "There are no heroes. There can't be heroes in Our Land."

Jack lost his patience. "*Look*, do you or don't you want to overturn the felines? So far," he continued in an irate tone, "all you've done is present a hundred excuses for not doing anything. What is it that's holding you back?"

"I-I-I don't know if it will work," I muttered.

"Well, you won't ever know unless you go ahead, will you?"

"I'm scared of the risks," I added.

"Well, life in this beautiful land is one big risk, isn't it? Adding another won't make a difference."

Finally, I confessed, "I don't think I'm up to it."

With that, Jack sighed, pursed his lips, ran his hand through his hair and rose to his feet. He towered over me. He looked down at me for a few seconds and said, "The spirit is willing but the flesh is weak, eh!" Then he walked away.

 My physical condition improved. I walked or rather, hobbled. My hind leg was still sore. It would soon be time for Jack and myself to part ways. He expressed his intention of resuming his travels in a few days' time. Jack had sowed a seed within me during the time I shared with him. What it was I did not know as yet, but that something was growing inside. Those few days were the birth pangs of a new life. A new glistening white kitten had been born within me. As I was a tabby cat, my peel was streaked grey. I did not like the colour; I never felt comfortable within my peel because it was a constant reminder of the dull greyness of my personality. I always admired white peels. It was a pity they rarely remained clean white. With time, they became irretrievably dirty and grey. Would the bright whiteness of this kitten be preserved? Could the outer ugly grey peel protect the kitten from the murky threats of oppression?

I turned over Jack's conversations in my mind. I regurgitated his truisms and wrestled with them. Jack had remarked that any institution, no matter how mighty, had a weak spot. The challenge was to find that weak spot and to exploit it. The superpower would then crumble. He maintained it should not be too difficult to identify the weak spot. That surprised me. Jack insisted it would be more challenging to unite the disenfranchised animals and the other kingdoms into one effective massive unit. It had to be a compact and compatible unit of incompatible elements that was to function as one. How was that possible?

I contemplated these ideas for days. Finally, I acted. Whatever induced me to do what I did? Frankly, I did not have the nerve to do it. It must have been the work of the white kitten within.

III

The cats had a crucial place in the organisation of the land. They were the messengers between the Overlords and all other animal groups in the land. It was one of their many dangerous menial jobs. I put these connections to good use.

I scrawled a message to the leaders of the myriad animal clans. I announced that an erect two-legged visitor was among us. This visitor spoke our language. He was willing to discuss ways of improving our quality of life. The visitor was prepared to discuss how to overthrow the Kingdom of the Felines.

The initial response to the reception of the communique was unenthusiastic and sceptical. That came as no surprise. However, on the day of the meeting at the W- shaped tree, the massive turnout astounded me. There were many representatives from almost all the animal groups.

What encouraged the animals to converge in droves by the W- shaped

tree? Was it because of the promise of a better quality of life? I doubt it. What made them accept an invitation by the universally ignored and derided leader of the cats? By then, the word had spread about my miraculous recovery. Such a recovery as mine never happened before. Nobody deemed it possible. The news must have caught the animals' attention. Did they turn up to witness the result of my resurrection? Possibly. They might have wanted to verify with their own eyes. More likely, they were curious to see what the two-legged, learned visitor looked like. In that, at least, they proved to be more curious than cats.

It was a sunny day with a gentle refreshing breeze. As far as the eye could see, the plain was packed with animals. It must have been the largest gathering of animals in history. The animal audience was respectful and attentive. There was a reverent aura associated with the meeting. It was interactive and conducted in a similar fashion to my discourses with Jack. The speaker's rhetoric resonated with the crowd as it had done with me.

Jack's message must have jolted these self-pitying, defeatist personalities. At the same time, however, he fascinated and inspired them to a higher ideal. Jack postulated that it might not be possible to defeat their masters in open battle. However, there were means of weakening their rule.

"Let the Feline Kingdom rule," he said, "but you can drive a wedge into it. You can then thrive safely within that wedge and concentrate on making that wedge as big and accommodating as possible."

He insisted that it was possible to divide the felines against themselves. We had to maintain the divisive pressure. The different feline factions in time would turn against each other.

The unity of the oppressed subjects of the felines was paramount. The various animals had to employ their unique skills in this type of subversive warfare.

The animal representatives became increasingly enthused. They liked what they heard. I picked up murmurs in the crowds like, "Nobody has ever spoken like that before," or, "What he says makes perfect sense," or, "He makes it sound so easy," or, "Why did we not think of it ourselves? What are we waiting for?" On my part, throughout this daylong conference, the inner white kitten matured into a young bright white cat.

By the end of the day, the arguments were exhausted. The meeting was about to be disbanded. The animals were preparing for their long journey home. But, I had that odd, intuitive moment. It was an initiative that must have originated from my inner white cat. It had come of age within me.

I proposed we vote for the election of Jack as our General. After the initial collective gasp of surprise that punctured the silence, the response was immediate, unanimous and monumental. A concerted roar of approval resounded throughout the land. It rocked the heavens above. It must have drowned out King Roar's pathetic, fearful roar. What did King Roar make of it? Little did he know that our roar of defiance was the signal for the resistance movement to race out of the starting blocks. But the hurdles ahead were too high for my liking.

George the fox was silently pensive throughout. He knitted his brows together. He mechanically rubbed his jaw with one paw throughout the discussions. He was conspicuous by his failure to participate in the general roar. When the leaders of each animal group came forward to cast their official vote, George was the last to cast the consenting vote. At the end of this long day, the vote to appoint Jack as their General was unanimous. Even the donkeys voted in favour.

From that day on, we referred to Jack as General Jack. His name was on everyone's lips. He became a household name. He was our rallying point.

General Jack predicted there would be a groundswell of sympathy and support from all the other animals of the land. And so it was!

What made General Jack abandon his cherished travel plans to live among us? In later years I too, pondered the question. It all boiled down to the Call of the Siren. He once explained to me that a siren was a beautiful mythical creature who sang a plaintive song. This sound enticed travellers towards her, where they then, made their home. The lure of that song was irresistible. Suddenly, it made sense. Jack heard my dying *cri de coeur* during his travels. He recognised the anguished sound for what it was – a desperate cry for help. It wrenched his tender heart. He could not resist the call. This incident foreshadowed another incident I had just unwittingly precipitated - the spontaneous collective *cri de coeur* of the non-feline animals at the assembly. It was the poignantly, thunderous cry for help from denizens yearning for release from bondage. Again, Jack could not resist such an appeal - that Call of the Siren.

The three interventions - my dying *cri de coeur*, my unlikely invitation and my equally unlikely nomination of Jack as General, were the three inciting incidents that were to change the destiny of the animal world for eternity. In truth, the latter two were not really my initiatives but those of the growing white cat within. Part of me regretted the third initiative which was to seal the fate of the animal world forever. There were rowdy scenes of jubilation right after General Jack's election. However, there was a tiny insignificant island of unquiet sadness within that otherwise seamless sea of jubilation. It was I. Was it normal?

My innate grey cat cursed me for what I had done.

"What have you done?" it said.

"Whatever got into you?" it continued. *"You can't do it. You don't have it in you. What have you let yourself in for?"*

"You were so safe and comfortable before". That grated.

In the midst of the amazingly joyous scenes around me, fears and doubts abounded in that tiny isle. The animals danced and rejoiced. I fretted in silence. My protective shell had been broken forever. I was now out in the open, exposed. The darkness of the uncertain path ahead was scary.

CHAPTER 3

ESPIONAGE

I

General Jack convened regular meetings with the leaders of the Four Kingdoms. He said it was essential to maintain a good communication system. For this, we relied on the birds of the sky. They were happy to oblige. They proved to be good scouts.

We also needed to obtain intelligence concerning the behaviour and habits of our Overlords. That is where us, cats came in because of our close relations with our fierce cousins. We were the only ones able to secure that delicate inside information.

It was also essential to make overtures to other animals, like the rodents and monkeys for assistance in conducting special ops.

We set up a chain of command. General Jack was the field commander. I was his *aide- de-camp* and the head of the secret service. The leaders of each group of the Four Kingdoms were subordinate to us but they supervised their own troops. They had their own designated responsibilities and duties.

The general enthusiasm grew. Animals from outside the Four Kingdoms volunteered their services. It was just as General Jack had predicted. There was plenty of good will to go around. The spirit of comradeship spread through the land like wildfire. Each day brought thousands of new recruits. The new *zeitgeist* united us, despite our diversities and rivalries, against a common detested enemy.

We called our organisation the Union Jack. We had our own symbol. There were two brown sticks in the form of an upright cross. One stick represented faith, the other hope. Two other green sticks in the form of an "X" were superimposed on the original cross. One green stick stood for courage, the other stood for friendship. The four sticks met at one point in the centre of life. General Jack explained those were the four ways of life. Provided the members did not stray from these paths, they would remain united and safe.

General Jack and I were the most senior members of the Union Jack organisation. The cats convened to appoint the twelve Union Jack division commanders. Scratchy and I were roped in by enthusiastic popular consent. We were the first natural choices, as were a few of my cousins and nephews. The election of each commander was noisily accompanied by the rhythmic banging of drums and intermittent cheering. Others volunteered. Some were accepted, others were rejected. Sabine was the first to volunteer but she was rejected on the premise that she was not steely enough. She was far too feminine and graceful to bark orders to the ungainly, rough and tumble troops.

In the end, we were one division commander short, though. That was the dispatch division post. The crowd speculated loudly on the profile of the putative holder of this post. It had to be someone with good communication skills. To our surprise, a strange cloaked cat came forwards to volunteer. We all stared hard at this mysterious stranger, because of his fascinating demeanour. The voice though, was familiar to me. I saw through the disguise. The silky, suave voice gave the stranger away.

It was Sabine again! She had no place amongst the uncouth agents. She was thrown out of the assembly, kicking, screaming, scratching and biting.

We were still at an impasse. We were about to noisily pack up but silence descended on the assembly, when Purr diffidently made his way to the podium. He stood up on his hind legs and twiddled nervously with his tail. He looked up at the General imploringly and softly said, "P-P-Please sir, can I be the chief dispatcher?" There was a loud murmur of disapproval throughout the ranks. I heard the scattered sniggers, contrived coughs and sarcastic sighs. In the end, Purr was recruited out of respect for his newly esteemed father. Besides, we were not exactly spoilt for choice.

Sabine sulked all day. Scratchy tried to console her with little success. She only shed her blues, when he spontaneously created a post of deputy for her in his department. To hell with anyone who objected to it, he declared. The impromptu posting was indeed, officialised. Sabine leapt with joy. They proved to be a dynamic, livewire duo. They conceived and executed a series of brilliant espionage missions.

All this happened under the noses of our Overlords. We were so secretive, they had no inkling of these exciting developments.

II

The structure and organisation of the resistance movement was set up. Now, we had to spring into action. General Jack wanted to infiltrate the headquarters of the King. There was a collective gasp of astonishment when he brought up the item on the agenda. No one had ever dared trespass in the lion's den. Nobody in his right senses would volunteer. Even if someone managed to enter the lion's den, he would never come out alive. It was a suicidal mission.

General Jack waved our objections aside. This was to be a mission for our rodent friends. A mole had to burrow a tunnel leading to the interior of the headquarters. Once opened, a mouse had to enter and look around for secret documents. I had told General Jack the rulers occasionally organised meetings on rule of law matters. They sometimes documented their discussions on paper. General Jack was interested in that type of intelligence. **(Page 181,#10)**

On the day, Manny the mole dug the tunnel. On emerging, to his horror, he was only a few inches away from the jaws of the sleeping King. The tunnel exit reeked of the lion's foetid breath. Manny froze in a cold sweat. His whiskers moved with each of the King's breaths. The King's

43

mouth was loosely open. The intimidating fangs were visible and Manny trembled. Nobody who came so close to those fangs ever lived to tell his tale. Manny's mouth dried up but after a few dozen measured breaths, he managed to compose himself. Manny tiptoed his way back into the safety of the cosy tunnel. Once inside, he silently extended it by a few metres.

We gave the green light signal for entry into the tunnel. Maxi the mouse was spot on. He deftly and silently explored the room. The King was snoring so loudly, Maxi's shuffling was drowned out. He found the ledge on which the papers rested. As he was about to jump onto it, the King moved. This electrified Maxi on the spot. He held his breath. The King snored on and his eyes remained closed. Maxi was safe. Maxi scampered on the ledge with stealth. He nervously alternated his glance between the papers and the lion. The ledge smelt of dried blood. Blood stained paws had officially stamped the papers. Maxi caught a glimpse of the relevant papers. They were conspicuous because they were the only ones of green vellum. I had briefed Maxi with the details before the mission. A skull was resting on top of this document as a paperweight. Maxi had to shove this skull to retrieve the document. The skull noisily jerked. Maxi's heart stopped. He looked at the King. The King's eyes were half open and Maxi recoiled in terror. The lion fixed his gaze ominously on Maxi. Silence descended on the room... Lub Dub... Lub Dub...Lub Dub...Lub Dub...The sound of Maxi's thumping heartbeat filled the room. The King's snores were no longer audible and his incredible hulk expanded to fill the room. Maxi tensed his muscles. He was ensnared. He weighed his chances. The window was closed. The lion's huge frame obstructed the path to the door. Maxi's sole chance was the second exit, which was equidistant from both him and the King. If he made it to the tunnel before the King, he would be safe out of the lion's reach. Once in the tunnel, he could easily escape from the camp. Maxi glanced at the towering lion. His eyes were still fixed on the ominously still, dark frame of the King. King Roar was about to pounce. Maxi crouched and drew a deep breath, bracing himself for the dash. Strangely, the sound of the heartbeat receded. The sound of snoring overdubbed the sound of Maxi's heartbeat. Maxi glanced at the King. The King was snoring but his eyes were still fixed on Maxi. How was that possible? The plucky mouse gingerly moved inch by inch to the other end of the ledge. At no point did he dare detach his timorous eyes off the King. The King's eyes did not follow him. They were fixed on empty space. Maxi let out a silent sigh of relief. He was safe after all. The King had not awakened. He merely slept with his eyes half open. Maxi rolled up the document and escaped with it through the tunnel. Mission accomplished!

Maxi delivered the documents to me as I waited outside at a safe distance, just outside the lions' camp. Maxi, the newly crowned hero, whispered to me that he saw the real crown on a ledge. He was tempted to steal that as well.

Then came a bolt from the blue.

By then we had reached the safe zone on our way home and I thought aloud to Maxi, "Wouldn't it be great if we had laid our hands on the King's crown? It would provide a huge morale boost for our fledging cause!" I sighed absently. Of course it was wishful thinking on my part, but it sparked off an inconceivable train of events.

Another young sprightly, ambitious mouse named Midi overheard me. He interpreted my words literally and seriously took them to heart. Midi impulsively tore away from our group that was returning home. Midi the mouse entered the warm, humid tunnel. He was not aware that there were two exits for the tunnel. Midi emerged from the dangerous first exit, straight into the jaws of death.

General Jack lamented the first casualty of our nascent campaign. He was disturbed. He insisted that everyone was to follow orders to the letter. We could not afford any more lapses. The success of the entire campaign hinged on keeping the felines in a state of blissfully ignorant complacency. It was crucial. We never realised how difficult it would be to operate behind an unbreached veil of secrecy.

General Jack was satisfied with the findings of the mission. The results were ground breaking. Henceforth, we referred to that mission as the "Day of Initiation".

We discovered that the lions and tigers hated and feared each other. We also discovered that the lions did not trust the jaguars, cougars and panthers. If the opportunity arose, the lions would not hesitate to wage war on them separately.

It was also revealed how friendly the lions were with the cheetahs and leopards. These two feline groups in turn, were submissive and loyal.

These were the fault lines in the Feline Kingdom. It was the kingdom's weak spot. That was our target. We had to exploit that weak spot. General Jack decided we had to widen those fissures rendering them permanent.

We resolved to divide the feline clan into three opposing rival fractions.

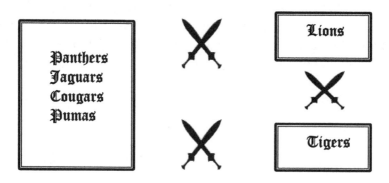

The General gave new instructions to the Union Jack cats. Covertly, they had to reveal the contents of those minutes to the chiefs of the tigers, cougars, panthers and jaguars. We had to perpetrate and intensify the reciprocal distrust between them and the lions.

We were about to stoke the fires of discord within the Feline Kingdom.

CHAPTER 4

THE DRAWING OF THE LINES

I

eneral Jack decided on the next mission. We now had to develop enmity between the cougars, jaguars and the panthers on one side and on the other side, with first the lions and then, the tigers separately. The primary objective was to split the Feline Kingdom into three warring armies

The grand mission was a series of twinned missions. Scratchy and Sabine together devised and directed these missions. The stakes were high. We studied every minor detail of the mission to improve the chances of success. Our homework was crucial. It involved the input and co-operation of many different animals.

Subversion was the name of the strategy. Would it bear fruit?

II

We planned six missions initially. The General approved of Scratchy's and Sabine's plans. These were co-ordinated by the cats of the Union Jack. They worked closely with the magpies whose aerial surveillance of the camps provided indispensable intelligence. The format of the operations was similar. In each mission, the cats wore leaf shoes on their four paws so as not to leave any footprints at the scene of the crime.

We focused initially on the tiger versus the panther/cougar/jaguar axis.

We selected the appropriate day and time of the operation in advance. There was a weeklong blood tournament involving all four feline groups. They attended these keenly fought tournaments. We anticipated the mass emptying of the respective feline headquarters barring the occasional guard. Scores of cats infiltrated the areas surrounding each feline camp. They hid in the trees and operated as sentries. At noon, the cats entered to inspect the camp. They had free access to undertake their usual mundane chores, so their incursions seemed perfectly natural to the Overlords. No suspicions were aroused. The inspection revealed that the tiger chief's house was unoccupied and that there were no guards. There were only four tigers in the entire camp, two of whom were sick and resting. The other two relaxed at fixed points in opposite ends of the camp. The timing was right. The way to the tiger chief's hut was free.

A large group of willing skunks was smuggled inside the tiger chief's quarters where they sprayed their pungent scents. After the smirking skunks did their work, they smugly slipped out of the camp silently and undetected. Meanwhile, a group of cats deleted the skunks' footprints with big leaves. Another group of cats was in possession of the four paws of a dead cougar. With these, the cats made footprints leading to and from the chief's headquarters. They also made these imprints within the tiger chief's hut.

At the same time in another site, we repeated the same process with a different set of personnel. The location was the cougars' headquarters; the objective was the home of the cougar chief. The purported perpetrators were the tigers. There were a couple of unsuspecting cougars lazing about, but otherwise the camp was deserted. Our Union Jack infiltrators ascertained this. The extensive network of sentries reported the all clear. After the skunks completed their work, the imprints left inside and outside the cougar chief's house were the paws of a dead tiger.

It was all so easy. The reports we received the next day could not be better. The tigers blamed the cougars for the outrageous insult while the cougars blamed the tigers. The felines were proud and arrogant. They took such insults seriously. They considered an insult against their leader to be an insult against their race. This would not stop there. There were bound to be serious and dramatic repercussions knowing the ferocity of the felines.

On our part, we were euphoric. Including the Day of Initiation, we had now conducted three successful covert operations. We had achieved the mission's goal of antagonizing the tigers and cougars. We credited ourselves for our efficacy, discipline and preparation. However, we had to keep our feet on the ground. We could ill afford overconfidence. Focus and concentration were crucial. We had been lucky. More operations were to follow. It was significant though, that the animals were growing in confidence and self-belief. There was good co-operation between the agents. Everyone trusted each other because each animal knew that his or her survival depended on the survival of every other animal. That mutual dependence was our solid unifying bond. They maintained the secrecy and remained silent. Up to that point, we were sure no word about our acts ever reached the felines' ears. At the same time, the animals took pride in their missions. We were off to a good start. If our luck held out, General Jack anticipated that we would go from strength to strength. If on the other hand, we slipped, the consequences would be serious. Our overall resistance campaign would flounder if the felines outed us. Essentially, they would nip our resistance movement in the bud. The potential sequelae were unthinkable because the felines would exact a terrifying revenge.

The second pair of missions coincided with the last day of the tournament. We conducted the twin operations simultaneously in both the tigers' camp and in the panthers' camp. Tension was running high among the Union Jacks.

The tigers' camp was deserted. Surprisingly, not a single tiger was present in the camp. The tigers were the finalists and they had a good chance of being crowned champions. Hence, the absolute turnout. The gods smiled on us that day. In the morning, the cats sneaked into the tiger chief's hut a large number of pregnant hens. We covered their claws with leaf shoes. These happy hens laid a large number of eggs over both the floor and the bed of the tiger. In the meantime, the cats made imprints with the paws of a dead panther both inside and outside the tiger chief's house. The exhausted tiger chief champion returned at night. Wherever he waded, he created a slimy, slippery mess in his room and bed. It was a painful experience and he had all the knocks and bruises to show for it the next day.

Another group of personnel duplicated the same operation in the house of the panther chief at the same time. The Union Jack cats infiltrated and inspected the camp. The panther chief's hut was empty. However, seven idling panthers were scattered at different points in the camp. One of them was sleeping only a short distance away from the panther chief's headquarters. In whispers, the cats assessed their options. Should they abort the mission? It was risky. What if that panther woke up and raised the alarm? Or, should they wake him up and lead him on a wild goose chase away from the camp? We considered this option riskier as the commotion might alert the other panthers who were not too far off. In the end, we decided to proceed, but with hyper-extreme caution. We conducted the entire operation with bated breath. The hens' stealth was commendable. They knew what the outcome would be if they were caught. On the other hand, the hens considered a successful mission to be the perfect tongue-in-cheek riposte to the felines. The hens would be avenging their systemic maltreatment in an exemplary way. Initially the mission proceeded smoothly. The hens did their part. They silently stole away. However, just after the cats had imprinted the incriminating paws of a dead tiger outside the panther chief's house, the nearby panther woke up. He sized up the three fidgety cats with his lazy gaze. The sheepish cats returned his gaze. Anything could happen now. Their hearts were in their mouths. At that instant, a large pelican irrupted into the scene with its colourful wide wings flapping. It deflected the panther's attention who could not resist the temptation. He sprung off in the bird's direction, chasing it out of the bewildered cats' range. The cats immediately fled in a state of shock. It was a close shave.

We had successfully completed even this pair of missions. However, we expected the worst. We anxiously waited for the reports on the aftermath. There was the foreseen bitter furore by the targeted felines over the twin incidents. The tigers blamed the panthers and the panthers blamed the tigers. There was now mutual aversion between these two feline groups. The panthers filed no report about the cats' presence in the camp at the time of the crime. We were stupefied and relieved in equal measure by this omission. We had been lucky again.

Two weeks later, we focused our attention on the tigers and jaguars. We opted for a day of blood sports involving both the tigers and the jaguars. In this sport, the respective chiefs selected ten fighters from each race for ten different fights. After the scuffles, the King counted the ten survivors of each fight. King Roar declared the feline race with most survivors the winner. The losing race had to pay homage to the winners.

The Union Jack cats infiltrated and surveyed the tiger camp. Ten tigers were scattered throughout the field. Some were asleep, others were awake but relaxing. The sentries outside reported that a couple of tigers were patrolling at a distance outside the camp. We had to alter our pre-planned homeward escape route because of these patrols. A large number of hedgehogs were ushered into the house of the tiger chief. They were safely inside when one of the tiger guards rose and prowled by the hut. His eyes met the terrified eyes of the three loitering cats who froze in fear. The tiger gazed at them indifferently. He showed no reaction and said nothing. He indolently continued his stroll out of the camp heading in a particular direction. The shocked cats pulled themselves together. The tiger's outward direction induced us to divert our homeward escape route again. Immediately after this heart stopping moment, the cats quickly made the imprints in the ground using the paws of a dead jaguar. They took off in a panic, abandoning the hedgehogs in the tiger chief's hut.

The tiger chief returned at night to sleep in his bed. When he crossed the threshold, a black curtain of bats descended upon him as planned. They covered his eyes and nose. There was no way he could displace them, not even with his claws. The room was swarming with a seemingly infinite legion of fast moving bats. His claws only tore into his face. As he struggled in agony, he fell on his bed of closed-up giggling hedgehogs. The tiger rolled in even more agony on this spiked floor. The hedgehogs then scurried out in the dark as the bats covered their escape.

At the same time in another place, different personnel conducted the same type of operation in the Jaguars' camp. The intended victim was the chief of the jaguars. We used the paws of a dead tiger as the incriminating clue. The camp itself was completely deserted. There was a posse of jaguars frolicking by a stream at a distance. Luck smiled on us. This operation went smoothly without incident.

However, that heart stopping moment in the tigers' camp had the potential of jeopardizing the entire campaign.

We waited anxiously for the expected backlash. Oddly, the tiger sentry made no report about the presence of the cats earlier that day. Yet again, the tigers and the jaguars blamed each other for the offences committed. The aggrieved victims never made the correct inference. They did not suspect the identity of the real offender. Our campaign was safe. Nevertheless, we had to be careful. The mission was still a work in progress.

It was too good to be true. We were thrilled with the outcome so far but the tension was becoming unbearably high. We knew our luck would not hold forever. It was only a matter of time.

Now we had to concentrate on firstly, the lion versus tiger clash and secondly, on the lion versus the cougar/jaguar/panther axis.

In the first pair of missions, the Union Jack cats found a lion cub born dead. They put tiger jaw marks all over its bloodied body. Two different Union Jack platoons executed both operations simultaneously in both camps. The chosen day coincided with the respective hunting day of both the lions and the tigers in the afternoon. We predicted the camps would be deserted. When King Roar was not at home, the cats planted the severed baby carcass in his hut. As usual, they left imprints of the paws of a dead tiger just outside and inside the hut. The same procedure was reprised in the tiger camp. This time the victim of the provocative act was the tiger chief. We deposited the dead tiger cub in a strategic place within the chief's residence. We impressed the footprints of a dead lion inside and outside the tiger chief's house. This was a relatively low risk mission, even though there were several bored residents who fortunately, were static and disinterested. Besides, they were spaced out at the far ends of both camps. The logistics were more straightforward and the execution of this pair of missions was faultless.

We were satisfied with the outcome. In fact, the mutual rage of the lions and tigers exceeded our expectations. The powerful tiger clan was particularly infuriated. They maintained that all the other felines were conniving against them. The lions suffered the outrage to their authority by their blood relations with festering rage.

We were in the clear.

The second and third pair of missions were more momentous and ambitious. We put our heads together and painstakingly plotted the logistics of these missions. We were patient. We waited for the right opportunity. We did not wait in vain, as we stumbled on the perfect diversion. A feline regal election was looming. It was playing out over a week. We could not ask for more. It was the ideal cover for our stealth operations. Two lion challengers to King Roar's throne had come forward. There were to be two fights to the death on two separate days, at the beginning and at the end of the week. We predicted that all the felines would set forth *en masse* from their camps on such an occasion given the high level of interest. On both days, it turned out the camps concerned were completely deserted. The saboteurs could operate furtively in relative freedom. We deployed many more Union Jack cats this time. We posted more sentries at many different points outside the circumference of the camps. They concealed themselves safely in the trees. Unlike the unpredictable monkeys, the cat sentries were discreet and trustworthy. The coast was clear as far as their eyes could see. For the second pair of missions, a mule volunteered to consume herbs. These distasteful herbs were renowned bowel irritants. Just after doing so, the leaf-shoed mule was shepherded into King Roar's headquarters. He discharged his pungent and profuse dung all over the place. The cats imprinted the paws of a dead jaguar outside. Another group of agents repeated the operation at the same time in the living quarters of the jaguar chief. The footprints outside were those of a lion.

We undertook the third pair of missions at the end of the election week. We infiltrated and surveyed the interior and exterior of the camps. Both camps were deserted. Our meticulous planning had paid off. For these missions, we recruited a grotty pair of hippopotamuses. A willing leaf-shoed hippopotamus demolished the entire house of King Roar from within and without. The cats had built it using trees, foliage, hay and mud. The entire structure caved in. The footprints around the ruins were those of a panther. Another detachment of Union Jack vandals undertook the same demolition job on the hut of the panther chief. The footprints outside were those of a lion.

We were ecstatic with the outcome. There were the reciprocal recriminations between the fierce feline groups. Our confidence was on a roll. Ironically, that was our undoing.

In the fourth pair of missions, our luck finally ran out. The lions caught us. Had we blown our cover? The cats led by Sabine conducted a group of leaf-shoed monkeys into King Roar's home. We gave them express orders to ransack the newly built house in a way that only they could. They made a dirty mess of it. The cats left the footprints of a cougar outside the hut. However, the King returned earlier than expected. The sentries outside caught a glimpse of the running King followed by his retinue. His final burst of acceleration did not permit

enough time for the sentries' message to filter through to all the operators around the King's home. The cats made a quick exit from the camp in time. The lions did not pick them up. The monkeys were caught unawares. They were trapped inside and panic set in. The unsuspecting

King Roar stopped a few metres from his home and turned to give orders to his subordinates. The entombed monkeys frantically gouged out an opening in the farther wall of the house. One by one, they scurried out unnoticed. They escaped unscathed from the camp before the King could react. King Roar's outraged roar, when confronted by the inside mess, echoed throughout the camp. The fleeing monkeys were still within earshot, but they were safe.

The King's rage was directed against the cougars.

III

A few days later, we repeated the same process. The location was the abode of the cougar chief using the footprints of a lion both inside and outside the hut. Here tragedy struck. Two brothers Chimp and Champ led the five monkeys. The cat steering them was one of my sons, Scratchy. The job was completed but the  monkeys were too loud and unruly. They indulged themselves so much, they overstayed despite Scratchy's loudly whispered entreaties. The noise caught the attention of the cougars lurking nearby. A trio of curious cougars approached to investigate. They took the saboteurs by surprise. The vandals were caught red-handed. One of the cougars caught Scratchy and pinned him down to the ground. The other two cougars tore up four of the monkeys but they could not apprehend Champ who slipped away unharmed.

Champ returned to our headquarters to report. He was breathless and distraught. General Jack immediately dispatched a group of magpies to  spy on the cougar's camp. While the spying birds were away, he assembled a rescue party. The magpies reported that all four monkeys were dead. Scratchy was held captive. The cougars mauled him badly. They tied him to a tree at the south pole of the camp. During the violent interrogation, Scratchy revealed he was working for the lions. He claimed that King Roar had recruited the group of saboteurs. He also alleged that the King himself had given him specific orders for the mission.

The cougars were not convinced, so they planned to visit King Roar with their prisoner the next morning. Both the King and the cougars had to verify Scratchy's story.

The rescue party had to move fast before this verification occurred. General Jack himself led it. He carried a torchlight from the fire he had produced out of two dry sticks earlier in the hot summer day. As the cougars were sleeping, he set fire to the dry vegetation and to a couple of huts. We did this first outside the southern entrance of the camp only a stone's throw away from where Scratchy lay. We then set fire to the southern part of the camp interior, not too far from Scratchy. The fire rapidly spread. As the entire cougar camp woke up, they all fled northward away from Scratchy. This mass panic exodus conceded a free path for the release of my son. A trio of chipmunks cut through the thick ropes that bound Scratchy.

The mission was a success. Scratchy's story remained uncontested because the cougars never visited King Roar. The unexpected bonus was that the cougars now blamed the lions not only for the sabotage, but also for the rescue fire.

All the covert sabotage missions had been completed successfully. The various felines blamed each other for the vandalism. Disquiet prevailed within the Feline Kingdom. The identity of the real perpetrators remained unknown. Our cover was surprisingly still intact.

Sadly, success came at a high price. My son died from his injuries three days later. I was crushed.

How I mourned my younger son! I had always been proud of him. He was a feline prodigy. He was everything I was not. I admired him from a distance. He was imaginative and there was no one in Our Land whom he could not outsmart. He was not in the habit of eternally weighing up the odds like I did. If something had to be done, he just did it. Moreover, he was a master of improvisation. In short, he was a natural. It was in his character to outwit his torturers by misleading them at a critical juncture. In so doing, he saved our entire campaign. I was grief stricken for many days. His death left an aching void for the rest of my life. It was only in my later years that I managed to fill that gaping void to some degree.

A well-attended memorial was organised to commemorate the five fallen heroes of this mission. In the front line opposite General Jack and me was Champ. He did not take his stony gaze off us throughout the ceremony. He blamed both of us for his brother's untimely death. This episode would return to haunt us at a later crucial time.

IV

Scratchy's death affected Sabine badly. Her whole life was centred around him. He was her point of reference. Scratchy was at the spearhead of all the Union Jack operations. Where he was, there she was by his side. The secret agents used to say, "You could not have one without the other," or, "You ask for Scratchy, you get Sabine. You ask for Sabine, you get Scratchy." She was in the thick of it, as Scratchy was. It was their way. They were comrades-in-adventure. Deprived of her alter ego, Sabine's world collapsed. It came hot on the heels of the slaughter of her family. Part of her died on the day of Scratchy's death. She cut herself off from the world. She stopped talking and refused to eat anything. She stared at the wall all day and never slept. She was a wreck. Twinkle mollycoddled Sabine in her overbearing way. It did Sabine no good. Purr was always there, silently helping in his understated way. He stood in the shadows unseen, never taking his protective eye off her. You could always rely on him. He was there when you needed him. I was of no use to her. I would have drowned in my sorrows were it not for the onerous tasks of the Union Jack organization which I continued to supervise.

After a few weeks, the green shoots of a tenuous recovery became apparent. She whispered her first words. She asked for food. She washed herself (previously, Twinkle washed her). She became aware of Purr's presence and she spoke her first words to him ever. "Thank you," she told him when he handed her the umpteenth dish he had helped Twinkle prepare for her. He carried her out in the fresh air because she was too weak to stand. She asked him to carry her to Scratchy's grave. He satisfied any whim of hers without a murmur of dissent. He lived for her. Sabine came to depend on him more and more, but like everyone else, she took

60

Purr for granted. He gave unconditionally; he never expected anything in return.

After a couple of weeks, Sabine became independent, though she dropped out of the Union Jacks.

One day, she was watching Purr drilling his troops. I joined her. She was thoughtful.

"Sabine, you're looking brighter every day. At this rate, in a few days' time, you'll be dazzling us again."

She feigned a smile. "How long has Purr been doing this for?"

"Oh! Since the day we founded the Union Jacks."

"I never noticed."

"You never noticed anything other than Scratchy. Welcome to the real world, Sabine. Open your eyes."

Purr had joined the Union Jacks to compete with Scratchy for Sabine's attention. He advanced in his own style, slowly, patiently and cautiously. He was respected even though he never really shone. Scratchy was brilliant. You could always rely on him to get out of a tight spot or for some spectacular feat. But you could not rely on him for the daily nitty-gritty, run-of-the-mill jobs. This is where Purr excelled.

Sabine had many admirers. She was well known in the Union Jacks, not only because of her good looks. She was a strong, vivacious character on a par with Scratchy. She made heads turn and tongues wagged. Scratchy's death changed her. She lost her cheeky, mischievous streak. She became more introspective and subdued. I was relieved to see that she spent more time with Purr. He was her tower of strength. They went for walks together. She enquired about his activities in the Union Jack. She prepared things for him. Days passed and her previous indifference evolved into gratitude. Weeks passed and her gratitude evolved into appreciation. Months passed and her appreciation evolved into admiration for Purr. With the passage of time, a mutual self-giving friendship developed. It was a platonic relationship. It could not be otherwise, or so I thought.

One day, Sabine called on me as I was eating. "Papi", she said, "What happens to the green hill and the green valley?"

"They come together as one, forever."

"*Exactly*, I am the hill, Purr is the valley and naught shall come betwixt."

I spluttered my drink (in her face). I was stunned by the realisation that their relationship had grown into something else. "W-what does Purr say?"

"He doesn't know anything. I know that it's what he wants, but he will never say it. On my part, it is what I want. Arrange the union now, Papi."

I said nothing. I slowly shook my head. I averted my eyes.

"*Please*, Papi. If not for me, do it for Purr."

I looked back into her upturned wide-eyed, beautiful face. I was moved, but still not to the point of unreserved conviction. Sabine always had that softening effect on me. Such was my devotion to her, I was like putty to her deft paws. She could mould me into any shape she wanted. But there was the other side of the equation to consider. The stakes were much higher than merely satisfying a passing innocuous whim of hers. Like Scratchy, Sabine was unpredictable. She was forever pulling rabbits out of her hat. You never knew what she's pull out next. A hedgehog, maybe?

"But, how can you say that? You're on the rebound, you're vulnerable emotionally. You'll do something you may later regret. You and Purr, you're as different as the sun and the moon."

"Not at all, I've never seen things more clearly."

"But you were hopelessly in love with Scratchy. You can't take Purr by default. It's not fair on him."

"I *thought* I was in love with Scratchy. I was attracted to him the first time I set my eyes on him. He was the mirror image of me. I liked and loved the reflection of myself. It was *myself* I was in love with, not Scratchy. I was so vain. Papi, your family has given me everything. I cannot ask for more. The family's character is epitomized in Purr. I love the family. Purr is the best embodiment of the family I love so much. I want to start giving. I want to experience the daily joy and satisfaction of giving. There is no one other than Purr, with whom I want to share these joys. I know you think I'm a scatterbrain, Papi. But trust me just this once. You won't regret it."

"Sabine, you don't know it, but I once made a heart-to-heart promise to your mother. That promise was sealed in the blood of my wife and your dying mother. It means the world to me. I intend to keep it well beyond my dying breath. You are my responsibility. I only want what's best for you. *But,* I have to think of Purr."

I played the devil's advocate. "Purr is so dull and colourless. You'll get bored and tired of him. You'll inflict pain on him when you ditch him. You'll be too hot for him to handle and I don't want him to get burnt."

"There's enough of Scratchy in me for both of us. So, there'll never be a dull moment. As for hurting Purr, it's inconceivable. I wouldn't dream of it. I'd be hurting myself and you know me, Papi, my pain threshold is low."

"But you've only known Purr these past few weeks. You had never spoken to him before. You *don't* know him well enough."

"I've been living in the dark too long. Now that I've stepped into the light, I know what it was I was missing. Once in the light, I want to stay in the light forever. I was restlessly seeking a treasure in the wrong places, but the treasure was there all along under my nose. I just ignored it. I want security, and consistency. I want my comfort zone so that I can continue raising your family, Papi. This is not a spur-of-the-moment infatuation. It is a long, tortuous and painful journey of self-discovery that has brought me into the arms of Purr. Now I know - Scratchy was my dear brother-in-adventure and he will remain so forever. I will always cherish him and a part of my heart will always be reserved for him. Purr, on the other hand, is something altogether different, something grander. Papi, you told me to open my eyes. I have opened them and you know that I have an eye for beauty - that kind of inner beauty. Purr is unique. When I'm with Purr, I'm in the company of a grey tabby cat with the assiduous heart and soul of a shepherd dog. What more can I ask for?"

Something moved inside me but still, I was not convinced.

Sabine continued to pressure me for an answer. She knocked on my door every day but I could not make up my mind.

I spoke to Purr in confidence. "I asked him why he was so smitten by Sabine from the day he set eyes on her.

"I-I-I saw Scratchy in her. H-H-He had everything I craved for, that I did not have."

"Then, why weren't you more forthright and forthcoming with her?"

" A-A-All I wanted was to support her and nurture her free spirit. I wanted to l-l-lift her up high so her light will shine brightly. I-I-I didn't want her flame to die out. T-T-The slow extinguishing of her flame pained me almost as much as Scratchy's death did. I-I- I did my best to keep it alight. I-I-I ask for nothing more."

The conversations finally dispelled any doubts I harboured. Sabine's future with Scratchy would have come to grief. It was fortuitous that the fatal mission was the only one in which Sabine and Scratchy were not side by side. Scratchy's bravery bordered on the reckless. Sabine's fate would have been no different to Scratchy's if she had devoted the rest of her life to him or someone of his ilk or indeed, if she continued on the same path alone. Committing herself to Purr's companionship would have been the ultimate fulfilment of my sincere promise to her dying mother. Sabine would be forever safe under Purr's secure, all-encompassing devotion. I'm sure that my wife and deceased children would have approved, as well.

General Jack consecrated the union with great pomp. Everyone was perplexed. What could the strong-willed, feisty belle see in dull and dour Purr? Both General Jack and I knew better, though. So did Twinkle, of all animals. She was overjoyed and she shed rivers of tears that day. Twinkle covered Sabine with kisses, complimenting her on her newfound wisdom.

The changes in Purr were remarkable. He gained in confidence and stature. He lost his stammer. He became more talkative, louder and articulate. His speech was assertive. There was a spring in his step. He laughed heartily and smiled profusely. He advanced in the Union Jack organization, becoming a captain. His devotion to Sabine blossomed, and the devotion was reciprocated hundredfold for the rest of their lives.

I always said that Sabine was full of surprises.

V

The results of the "Month of the Seven Missions" exceeded our expectations. Our masters are proud and arrogant beasts. When their dignity is effaced, they howl skyward with their bloodcurdling cry of vengeance. Moreover, their clan members rally around them as one.

The formidable tigers adopted a siege mentality against all.

The jaguars, cougars and panthers together gravitated towards the same side. They formed the second formidable group. This group closed its ranks against both the tigers and the lions (throughout the lions were loyally supported by

their cheetah and leopard cousins).

The lions closed ranks around themselves and their two fiercely loyal relations. This was the third, largest and most powerful group.

General Jack hinted that we had planted the seeds of an internecine feline war.

Subsequent events took an unexpected turn. Instead of turning against each other as we predicted, the three feline power groups reacted in an unusual way. The factions feared each other. They were evenly matched in strength. Rather than risk mutual self-destruction, they opted to migrate and settle as far away from each other as possible. The tigers migrated to the Western part of Our Land. The cougars, panthers and jaguars migrated to the Eastern part of Our Land. The lions and their allies settled in the Southern part of Our Land. The three factions anticipated that the long distance separation would protect them from a repetition of the guerrilla attacks sustained during the "Month of the Seven Missions".

Regretfully, these events were to prove our undoing.

VI

 By now, the young white cat within me had matured into a glorious fully-grown cat. Thankfully, it grew at the expense of the grey tabby cat. I was proud of it. I was pleased that it was in charge. Optimism and self-belief had substituted pessimism and diffidence. Industry and efficiency had supplanted indolence and ineffectiveness. Courage and initiative had trumped cowardice and inertia. Reliability and consistency displaced indecision and procrastination. There was competence where previously there was incompetence. I was pleased that the positive inner white cat dominated the negative outer grey tabby cat. However, that inner nagging feeling plagued me. Was it the real me?

To outside observers, I was the perfect leader. My idealism, restraint and industry complemented General Jack's wisdom, pragmatism and vision. My star rose as the white cat within matured. The non-felines held me with the same high esteem they reserved for General Jack. I was the co-founder and leader of the Union Jacks. My name was on everyone's lips. If anything, they related more to me than to the General, as I was one of them - a four-legged animal born and bred in the same land. Moreover, everyone had witnessed the transformation of my personality after my rebirth. Unbelievably, they regarded me with awe. No one knew my inner story. Even if they knew it, they would not comprehend it. For them, I was a new animal, a benevolent demigod. They delighted in the fruits of my bounty. I was the reason for all the good fortune. I was the architect of the successful missions. For how much longer could I go on with this pretence? The strain wore me down.

Inwardly, I knew that in my dual personality the white and the grey were in dynamic equilibrium. If one fell, the other rose to occupy the vacuum. These two inner cats were diametrically opposed. One was the antithesis of the other. I loved the white but I was ashamed of the grey. The problem was that the grey was the default mode. That was my liability.

For the time being however, I was satisfied with the chemistry. White Miaow wore a grey hair shirt on the outside. It served as a useful check. It prevented confidence becoming overconfidence. It prevented pride turning into arrogance. It prevented courage transforming into recklessness. It rendered me humble and modest. I had to agree I was the ideal foil to General Jack. We were in perfect harmony. I was his loyal sidekick. But again, deep down, it was not really me. I was completely reliant on General Jack. Without him, I was but a leaf fluttering in the wind.

CHAPTER 5

THE MUTINY

I

nother well-attended grand council was called. The crowd was excitable and the morale was sky high. General Jack took the floor. He claimed the victory was only partial. At least, we had an enclave of free space in which we could live, now that the Overlords had moved to the periphery. A loud cacophony of disapproval followed the General's statement. The crowd demanded full liberty. They were not satisfied with anything less. The more they achieved, the more they wanted. There was no limit to their appetite for liberty now. Their spirits and expectations were unrealistically high. General Jack admitted we had more work to do. We had to be patient. We were in it for the long haul, but we were on the right track. The Union Jacks had to persist with the provocative guerrilla tactics until the three factions reached their respective breaking points. A full-scale internecine war would ultimately break out between the felines. He predicted there would be no victors among combatants in such a war. The non-felines could then claim the land for themselves.

Despite our mishaps, fate had let us off lightly on the Day of Initiation and the Month of the Seven Missions. No one denied it. The overall success of our entire campaign, however, was dependent on keeping the felines in a state of blissful ignorance throughout. This warning was impressed on everyone. The felines' overconfidence was so haughtily complacent, the thought of brewing unrest in the land's undergrowth never crossed their collective mind. They would never have imagined any of us animals were capable of doing anything so audacious. Nor were they aware of General Jack's existence. A puny non-feline subject could not challenge the Feline Kingdom's authority. It was unthinkable for a fierce feline. This secure confidence of invincibility was the main reason for them failing to draw the lines between the dots. In the Month of the Seven Missions, they repeatedly missed the wood for the trees. Nevertheless, no matter how well prepared our missions were, mistakes were bound to happen. In no time, these separate errors would become a string of errors. This thread would become a connection. The connection would become a suspicion. The suspicion would snap into a shocking revelation. That revelation in the feline-dominated world would instigate the terrible reaction that we all dreaded. Although elation and overconfidence abounded in our ranks, there was a high degree of tension. This tinderbox was to set the stage for a series of unexpected events. The campaign was about to go down the path General Jack never intended.

II

 On my request, we adjourned the meeting for a couple of days. The General's speech was an anti-climax that satisfied no one. Discontent was brewing. I appointed the sparrows to gauge the various animals' reactions in secret. They had to report to me twenty-four hours later.

The reports, when they arrived, were disconcerting. The coalition was on the verge of breaking up. Different factions were taking shape among us.

The pacifists were content with what they had achieved and wanted to pack up. At least, the spatial distancing from the Overlords had now eased the pressures of mundane daily life. This pacifist group was composed of a large section of the animals that did not belong to the Four Kingdoms.

At the other extreme were the warmongers led by George the fox. These were in favour of all-out immediate total war. Their support came from the upper echelons of the Four Kingdoms.

In between these two extremes were the moderates, who I am sad to say, included the cats and the other lower classes of the kingdoms. These disagreed with the other two groups. However, they did not subscribe to General Jack's continuing plan of subversion. The missions had become too dangerous. The number of casualties was bound to continue rising. The felines would expose our illegal activities at some point. It was inevitable. The discovery would nullify all our previous accomplishments. This faction was in favour of suspending hostilities for the time being. They advocated a watchful waiting policy. We could relaunch the campaign at a later opportune time. Moreover, General Jack's prediction

of a civil war within the Feline Kingdom was far-fetched. The felines were too smart to risk mutual self-destruction.

The most worrying information however, was the emergence of the radicals led by the hot headed grey wolf Olaf. Their policy was the radicalisation of George the fox's plan. Essentially, the aim for them was the total defeat of the Feline Kingdom. Nothing must stand in their

way when it came to achieving that end. Any internal opposition had to be swept away, forcibly if need be. The biggest threat to achieving this end was General Jack, according to Olaf. The General had become a liability for the cause. He was the reason for the lack of unity in the coalition. He and his sidekick had to be disposed of. The means justifies the end. That was Olaf's motto.

I became concerned for the General's safety so I directed one of my sparrows to observe Olaf's movements throughout the day.

III

George the leader of the foxes took the floor when the council reconvened. He ridiculed General Jack's strategy.

"The General's strategy only managed to force the Overlords' retreat into their fortified positions," said George the fox. "At best, continuation of that policy will only entice the enemies to relocate their respective fortresses further away from each other. They'd still remain masters of the land."

He continued, "The situation would get even worse. Instead of one king, we'd end up with three kings each controlling its territory - a kind of co-federation of three despotic kingdoms loosely bound by the fear of mutual destruction. The other animals will still be victims of the felines' cold war."

The wily fox suggested General Jack's planned war of attrition had misfired. He implied General Jack outlived his usefulness. The animals were prepared to give General Jack an honourable discharge.

"The General has taken the resistance movement as far as he could. Someone more courageous must take over the leadership," he said, to loud cries of approval.

Next to me, General Jack rose to reveal he had a plan B about which he himself had reservations. He was drowned out by the boisterous commotion about him.

 George the fox then outlined the obvious military strategy.

"Never have the Four Kingdoms and their allies been so united in a common cause. It therefore follows that together we could form the largest army ever seen in the land. This army outnumbers the Overlords' army by 500,000 to 1. In addition, we have the element of surprise to our advantage. Our newly appointed leader could lead the great army into a *blitzkrieg* total war. First, we descend on the cougar/jaguar/ panther coalition in the East of Our Land. After wiping them out, we would then force march onto the unsuspecting tigers in the West of Our Land. We overwhelm those as well. With each victory, the great army becomes stronger as more animals swell its ranks. We then conclude the war by delivering the *coup de grâce* to the lions and their associates in the south."

The speaker became more excitable.

He shouted, "Us common animals, we have never been so strong. The Overlords have never been so weak and isolated before. They are too polarized. They can't help each other out. Divided they fall. My battle plan could not fail as long as we act decisively now. We have to strike while the iron is hot. Speed is crucial here. We must strike before the felines catch wind of our plans. The lightening campaign should be over in six days at the most."

There were cheers of approval and support from most animals in the assembly, even from the cats. General Jack sat silent shaking his head. I was the only other silent one next to him, surveying the general belligerent response across the floor. The animals had made their choice. They had all but chosen their new crafty leader. The General was isolated, but come hell or high water, I would never abandon him. After the commotion died down, I took the floor,

"Friends, I suggest we reflect on the new developments for a couple of days. We will reconvene for a final vote." Little did I know that this natural proposition of mine was to have such unexpected repercussions.

That vote could decide the fate of the animal world.

Embattled, General Jack strolled unnoticed all the way to his quarters where he slumbered. The huge crowd circled their new leader-designate, carrying George the fox shoulder high as they yelled war chants.

On that warlike note, we adjourned the assembly.

IV

George the fox sought us out a few hours after the adjourned meeting. He and his close associate requested a meeting with General Jack and myself privately at a secluded location by the river. They desired a negotiated compromise. The onus was on us to formulate a common strategy that was acceptable to all. The General was all in favour of this kind of diplomacy. We gladly accepted the invitation.

An hour before the scheduled *rendez-vous*, the sparrow tasked with shadowing Olaf the wolf returned. The details were sparse. Olaf was up to some mischief with George the fox that concerned both the General and myself. I was struck by that sinking feeling and I dashed off to warn

74

General Jack. On the way, Noisy the crazy parrot clattered into me. He blocked my path. He fluttered his colourful wings and made an endlessly repetitive din. As usual, I could not understand a word he said. Unexpectedly, he turned aggressive and he assailed me. He bit my ear with his long curved beak. Then he attempted to cut off my tail. I swiped him off with my paws. He reacted by biting my paw. Of all animals, the conspirators had sent this ridiculous bird to assassinate me. After a few minutes of struggle, I overpowered him and pinned him to the ground spread-eagled.

I was about to strike the mortal blow, when an authoritative voice shouted,

"Stop! What's up?" It was General Jack.

I unintentionally released my grip on Noisy. He evaded me and flew up onto a branch. From his high perch, he addressed the same repetitive din to the General. General Jack looked up, eyes and ears open. When Noisy eventually fell silent, General Jack put his arm on my shoulder.

He said, "Come on, let's go home. The meeting's cancelled."

As we walked home, I excitedly told him about the sparrow's latest report and of how I had just survived an assassination attempt. I hissed my scorn against the inadequacy of my assailant.

"Would you believe it, that clown even tried to chop off my tail?"

General Jack replied cryptically, "Don't judge by appearances."

His statement baffled me.

Many years later, I had an interesting conversation with Beady Eyes the owl.

I never forgot the conversation so I will relate it in Beady Eyes' own words.

"I had overheard a conversation between Olaf the wolf and George the fox. Olaf was determined to assassinate both you and General Jack. The scheduled meeting by the river was a trap. There were to be no discussions. There wasn't enough time. I could only avail myself of Noisy the crazy parrot to warn you about the danger. There were no other birds around. I myself, had to shadow these two conspirators. I knew that both you and the General were probably already on your way to the meeting place. The assassination was foiled through Noisy's timely intervention. Noisy then told me what happened. He said he managed to intercept you, but you couldn't understand what he was saying. You signalled your intention to wave him off and to continue your run to the meeting place.

You left him with no choice. He had to detain you physically. He did this to save you from a tragic fate. Luckily, the General intervened in the nick of time. He rescued Noisy from your aggression and almost certain death. It was also fortunate that the General understood Noisy's message. You could both easily return home safely."

"What was Noisy's message?" I asked.

"Olaf .... George.... kill.... Miaow....Jack."

This revelation humbled me. I sought out Noisy to make amends. By then, he had already left in search of the New Lands. Noisy the crazy parrot was not crazy, after all. My assailant was my saviour. He saved both my life and General Jack's.

General Jack once observed, "It's amazing. When you arrive at an impasse in your quest, decisive help arrives out of nowhere. It comes from where you least expect it. That must be a sure way of knowing you are on the right path."

Incredulously, I asked Beady Eyes, "How is it possible that even George the fox was involved in the plot? I know he's crafty and ambitious but he's not the violent type."

Beady Eyes replied, "It wasn't his idea. The idea originated from Olaf and his wolf pack. George didn't approve, though, he *did* try to cover it up because it was in his interest. He knew both of you were respected. He was planning to pin the blame for your murder on the Overlords. He wanted to engender widespread anger among the Four Kingdoms and the allies. That way, all the animals including the pacifists would unite in favour of George the fox's battle plan. He was prepared to sacrifice you as martyrs to achieve his end. He thirsted for the unity that was so essential for the success of his battle plan."

I could not understand General Jack. Why did he never tell me about our near death episode? Why did he never denounce both Olaf and George? The workings of General Jack's mind puzzled me at times but he was always right. Maybe he wanted to preserve the unity of our grand alliance at all cost? Fracturing that alliance would have jeopardized our struggle for freedom. But how could we maintain that unity if we had unscrupulous traitors in our midst? That worried me to no end.

V

The assembly reconvened in a confident mood. The vote was about to be taken with an expected unanimous result.

I took the floor. I looked in the General's direction. Our eyes met. The large crowd was in a lively, talkative mood. My presence on the podium was noticed. The chatter gradually died down, albeit for the scattered mumblings and the noisy clearing of throats. Unknowingly, I was to express yet another of my fateful statements.

"We can't take the vote until we hear General Jack's plan B."

The chit chat died down completely. The leaves rustled in the suspenseful silence. All eyes turned expectantly on General Jack as he took the floor.

"We have only one chance at victory. If we get it wrong, we are finished forever. The victors would exact a terrible revenge against whoever dared challenge their authority so brazenly. The Feline Lords will conduct a scorched earth policy from which we will never recover.

"The great army that my esteemed colleague George the fox speaks of, is a large mob not an army. It is not united. It can never be. It is divided by its very nature. It is a polyglot of disparate animal groups each with its own idiosyncrasies. All they have in common is their desire for freedom. That however, does not guarantee compactness and unity of purpose on the battlefield. By contrast, our masters' armies are compact and homogenous. They consist of one large animal group acting with one brain, one body and one set of limbs.

"You may outnumber them 500,000 to 1, but individually their fighting skills outdo yours by that same ratio. A cat has nine lives, but your masters each have a thousand lives. They will be next to impossible to kill. Your masters are born fighters. They fight to kill. You are not like that. What is to stop you, when you experience the initial fallout during the battle heat, from breaking ranks and fleeing? Your whole dream dissipated in a puff of dust! You would have tragically undone all our hard won achievements.

"You are basing everything on emotional wishful thinking. We need firmly cast battle plans."

The general sighed. He coughed and cleared his throat.

"It's true I have a plan B for open battle but even I have my reservations about it –"

"Let us hear it!" shouted the spell bound crowd.

"Fine, fine. Hear me out, then."

"One. We have to split into three armies. That will ensure we are more cohesive as a unit. The disparate groups of animals may then be easier to control.

"Two. We have to engage each enemy army separately *at the same time*. Our engagement has to be defensive. We have to use feints in order to draw the enemy into the opening attack.

"Three. We have to steer and manoeuvre each enemy army into a disadvantageous position on the battlefield. By then, our own armies should have already occupied the high ground that gives us the tactical advantage during the subsequent battle.

"Four. The composition of our armies has to be matched in strength and complementary to that of the enemy. It also has to be as uniform as possible.

"Five. Our different units have to perform a function that is compatible with the animals' characteristics. We require a heavy cavalry unit to overrun the enemy. We require a light cavalry unit to break the enemy ranks with feinting runs. We need to have both short and long range artillery units to harass the enemy armies.

"Six. Our main army will be located in the south against the most powerful enemy army consisting of the lions. The bulk of our army is infantry based and composed of weak troops. It will have to be shielded by an extensive network of lethal barrier traps.

"I have the battle plans in my mind but they are top secret. I can only present them to the division commanders at a secret Council of War.

"I told you I had my reservations. Battle plans can look grand and infallible on paper. Those factors I can control. What I do fear however, are the many variables that I have no control over. Ultimately, it is these unexpected twists of fate that determine the outcome of a battle."

I rose to take the vote.

The docile crowd exclaimed with one mystified voice, "What vote?"

That assembly was unique in that it ended with no binding vote. They had revved up into a crescendo for a momentous vote. My unforeseen instinctive intervention when I adjourned the assembly had again proved decisive. The militants' insane activism had been stunted. The reflective interlude I summoned had taken the wind out of the fiery warmongers' sails. The fate of the animal world lay in the balance now. General Jack quelled the rebellion with words. Was that another miracle? The field was now clear for General Jack. He had free rein to continue building upon the previous achievements.

What were these battle plans? Would they prove to be just hot air?

CHAPTER 6

THE COUNCIL OF WAR

I

General Jack opened the discussion. "Friends, you all said we were lucky on the Day of Initiation. What is luck? It does not just fall into our laps. We have to create our own luck. Through hard work and preparation, we construct a stage. We then invite Lady Luck to visit us and weave her magic spell on the stage. She may or may not be inclined to visit our stage. If she does, we are lucky. If she does not, then we are unlucky. It is certain however, that if we don't do our homework to the best of our capabilities, then we can never be lucky. We must strive to build as good a stage as possible in order to entice our beloved Lady Luck."

General Jack divided the battlefield into three areas- the West, the East and the South. **(Page 181, #2)** He etched the battle plans on the soil with a stick.

The aerial scouts had strict instructions to be at the site of action, never to take their eyes off the combatants on the battlegrounds wherever they were. They had to follow and observe every movement of each battalion, friend or foe. They were expected to provide the on-site intelligence to each leader on the respective battle field.

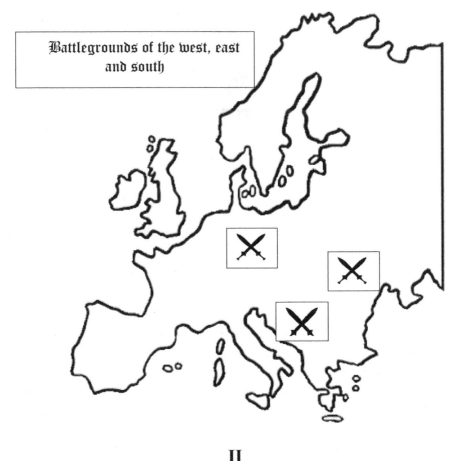

Battlegrounds of the west, east and south

II

The Army of the West was composed of two thirds of all the elephants in Our Land. They were to occupy a favourable defensive position on a hill facing eastward. One third of the elephants were to be deployed on the downslope. Only this segment of the army would be visible to the tiger army. The remainder of the elephant army behind the hill had to be concealed from the tigers' view. The split view was intended to mislead the enemy into underestimating the Western Army's strength. This would give the enemy a false sense of security. When in small groups, felines feared the elephant masses and avoided them. That is an acknowledged fact. Nevertheless, it was possible that they might be tempted into

82

attacking outright what they considered to be a vastly outnumbered elephant army. In such an event, that would be the signal for the unexpected devastating heavy cavalry counter-charge of the *entire* elephant army. This would overrun the charge of the outwitted tigers while in full stride, wiping all the tigers off the face of the earth once and for all. If the tiger army did not take the attack initiative, then Popo the elephant leader was to give the order for the full-blooded opening charge after receiving the Signal in the Sky.

Figure 1: The Army of the West

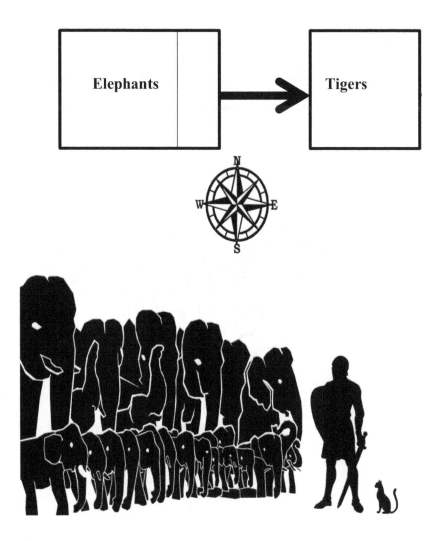

III

The Battleground of the East was a large open plain intended to favour multiple cavalry charges. These charges were to cross-link and reinforce each other in successive charges. However, the charging units were forbidden from overextending beyond the margins of the battlefield. **(Page 181, #1)**

The allied army was divided into three divisions grouped mainly according to their blood relations. The buffalo-led division formed the heavy cavalry on the northern flank. The elks and coyotes formed the weaker lancer division on the southern flank. These two flanking divisions were backed by the bulk of the central cavalry led by the awesome wolf pack and the grizzly bears. This latter division had all our shock troops.

The cougars, the pumas, the panthers and the jaguars made up the enemy army in this battlefield. Everyone knew that our masters feared the wolves, bison, buffalos and especially, the bears. These together, had to cover for the deficiencies of their weaker fellow fighters.

All divisions were to charge *en masse* from their respective positions *simultaneously* as soon as they received the Signal from the Sky. The differential speed of the various units in the allies' army would assail the standing feline army with wave after wave of continuous battering.

Figure 2: The Army of the East

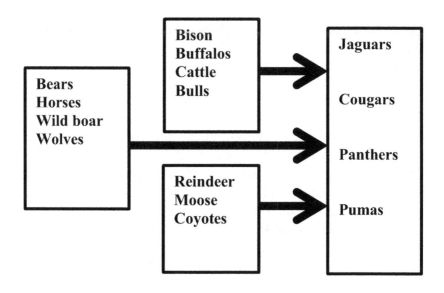

IV

The Army of the South was the largest army but contained the weakest troops of the entire grand alliance. This was the biggest, trickiest and most difficult battle. Our adversaries were the strongest here.

At the sight of the Signal in the Sky, the weak but swift light cavalry led by the gazelles was to run westward *towards* their comrades in the main army. The feigned retreat would act as the decoy to goad the lion army in hot pursuit. The powerful feline warriors would only see a weak enemy ahead of them. They would not hesitate nor resist the temptation to strike.

As soon as the lions charged, the heavy cavalry led by the rhinos had to mobilise. These were previously hidden in the forest. Once mobilized, they had to charge into the chasing lions from the rear and forcefully push the remaining felines into the fatal trenches further ahead. As soon as the escaping light cavalry prey led by the gazelles arrived within a few metres of the trenches, they were to bifurcate. They then had to continue their retreating run under the cover of the woods to join the flanks of their weaker companions.

The monkeys, gorillas and apes were the concealed artillery troops in the trees who covered the light cavalry's retreat. They had to pelt the lions with coconuts, stones, tree branches and whatever else they could lay their hands on.

The massed shield wall of horned pikes led by the stationary bulls and rams had to shield the main bulk of the army behind the trenches.

The Southern Army was a mix of troops from among the ones feared by the lions - (the elephants, hippopotamus and the rhinoceros) to the swiftest troops (the gazelle and the antelope); from the smartest troops (the monkeys) to the deadliest and most deceptive (the snakes in the trenches). Together, these troops had to cover the weak domesticated troops forming the bulk of the army in the rear.

Figure 3: The Army of the South

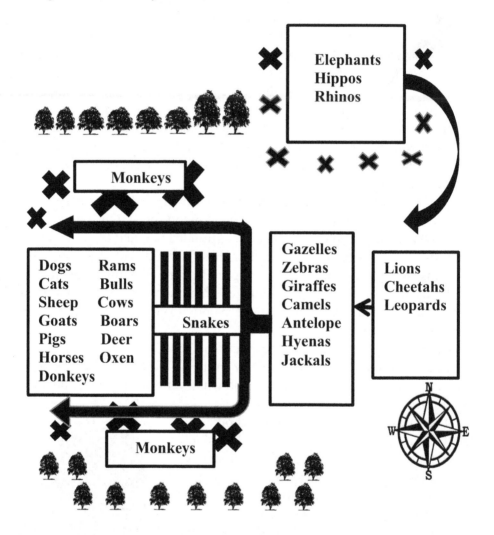

The chickens and rabbits, who were to be daubed in sticky mud, volunteered to leap into the mouths of the charging felines, thereby neutralizing their fangs. The defensive territory they were to occupy, had to be strewn with a carpet of broken eggshells and banana skins. The slippery grass was intended to throw the charging felines off balance. With the enemy thus unsettled and dazed, the vast mob of sheep, donkeys, mules, cows and horses were to crowd around the felines. As the lions struggled belly up on the ground, the allies had to clobber the felines with their hooves. This was a dicey battle tactic which the brave chickens themselves proposed. We had to see how their suicidal defanging mini-countercharge would pan out, but the chickens' resolve was ironclad. They maintained that they would die anyway; better to die fighting in the skirmishes.

We insisted that their exposed flanks were to be guarded by a large contingent of tortoises arrayed shell to shell. The shifting, unsteady surface they provided was intended to weaken the paw grip of the feline charge and to unbalance their rushed approach.

The commanders listened attentively. The close of the General's talk was greeted with nods and claps of approval. They became increasingly excited, punching the air in defiance and they all gruffly uttered one word. A loud discordant "aye" was heard far beyond the walls of our hut. A distant bystander could hear the drunken song coming from our hut:

"Crush, crush, crush, we crush 'em,
Crash, bang, boom, we crush 'em,
Crash, rush, flush, we crush 'em,
Crush, crush, we crush 'em, yeah!"

The division commanders took our victory as a *fait accompli*. I too, joined in this triumphant orgy.

When all was said and done, the next day we started our preparatory work. There was a feel-good atmosphere among us.

CHAPTER 7

PREPARATIONS

I

We consulted the birds of the sky. They were willing to participate. We needed them to scour the land, looking for suitable areas where the battles could take place.

The Crows reconnoitred the Western part of Our Land. **(Page 181, #3)** This was the easiest job as we were looking for a suitably positioned hill or ridge. The choice for the Eastern battlefield was not difficult. This was the responsibility of the eagles and hawks. The scouting of the Southern land was more taxing as the battleground had to be at the edge of a suitably positioned forested area. Our army had to be positioned within the curve of the U-shaped entrance of the forest, with the arms of the U providing cover for our army's flanks. Our scouts here were the cranes and falcons.

This mission was top secret. At all costs, the vultures were not to know of our battle plans. We did not trust them. It was in their interest to have a battle fought, but a feline victory was also in their interest. Everyone knew that if the felines won, the subsequent retribution would perpetrate the blood shedding to the vultures' delight. As far as the vultures were concerned, the more carrion the better

II

Our airborne scouts were satisfied with the territories chosen. General Jack whittled down the compiled short lists. We selected the three most suitable battlegrounds. We now turned our attention to the formation of a grand battle alliance. There was plenty of good will around and each battlefield had a good vibe about it..

We recruited the sapping animals: the moles, the meerkats, the groundhogs and the weasels. These excavated an extensive network of deep parallel trenches at the mouth of the U- shaped border of the forest in the southern battlefield.

The monkeys, apes and gorillas were delighted to be our artillery troops. Their brief was to convert the U, V, W or Y shaped trees into catapults for long-range firing. They were also to construct platforms in the trees flanking us. On these platforms, they had to stockpile any ammunition they found. True to their nature, they relished the prospect of this battle.

Next, we had the unsavoury task of approaching the slimy snakes. They too, were eager to play a part in this battle. The vipers, cobras, rattlesnakes and pythons volunteered. They had to occupy the camouflaged trenches into which the charging lions were expected to fall or be pushed into by our trailing heavy cavalry. The snakes could not wait to bury their fangs into the dreaded enemy. They would be proud of their grisly trophies.

We recruited three reliable white doves who were each to bear a giant reddish green leaf that would serve as the Signal in the Sky for battle commencement in each battlefield.

Finally, various birds donated differently coloured feathers. A large multi-coloured standard was constructed. We mounted this flag on the highest tree at the eastern border of the forest in the southern battleground. It was to serve as the reference point for the opening gazelle-led run.

III

The role of espionage naturally fell to the cats of the Union Jack. They were to operate as double secret agents. The cats furnished us with valuable accurate information about the state of the enemy including their plans, numbers and attitudes. Conversely, they provided the Feline Overlords with unreliable intelligence. **(Page182, #9)** The Union Jacks deliberately underestimated the size and composition of the allied army. They withheld from their Overlords vital information about the deployment of concealed units in the Western and Southern Armies. The cats exaggerated the low morale, discord and incompetence of the allies.

Their most important operation though, on the day of battle, was to act as the Overlords' scouts. The cats had to steer the three enemy armies into the disadvantaged areas of the respective battlefields that General Jack had reserved for them.

IV

 General Jack insisted on repeated rehearsals within the battlefields until he was happy that everything went smoothly. The most difficult manoeuvre to get right was the bifurcating gazelle-led run around the trenches in the Southern Battlefield.

We finally completed these training routines to the General's satisfaction. We were proud of our endeavours.

The military commanders reconvened in what was to be the final Council of War. The commanders were excited and optimistic. D-Day could not come a day sooner for them. General Jack alone remained silent and gravely thoughtful.

I took him aside and asked, "*What's* eating you, General?"

"I've got this gnawing feeling," he replied.

I retorted, "Surely, after all this, nothing can go wrong. After all the hard work and these rehearsals! I would imagine that we have won the battle before it even started. The rulers have no inkling of what is happening. They don't know about you. They will be unprepared, tired and surprised as soon as they set foot in the different battlefields."

Jack slowly replied, "You're not comparing like with like. Simulation is one thing. The battle itself is another. You cannot simulate true battle conditions in a training session. In the heat of battle, anything can happen. Everything is decided in a split second. On the battlefield, everything is done through instinct. You have to improvise accordingly. The problem is that we do not have one animal instinct in our army but countless different types of instincts.

That said, we reached the final lap - the official declaration of war.

CHAPTER 8

THE CASUS BELLI

I

eneral Jack used a difficult word. He wanted to provoke our rulers into declaring war on us. He did not want the allies to declare war. The division commanders could not understand the rationale for doing so. They regarded it as a waste of valuable time. They wanted to strike the felines in a surprise, all-out, full frontal attack as quickly as possible. As more time passed, the chances of the felines uncovering our secret activities increased. If they did so, it would be game over for us. For the commanders, the General's dilatory approach was a case of needless hair-splitting. What if the enemy did not take the cue and declare war? After all, that is indeed what had happened between the Feline Overlords after the multiple provocations during the Month of the Seven Missions.

General Jack was adamant that this was to be a defensive war at all costs. **(Page183, #5)**The success of the battle depended on luring the enemy armies into a trap. For the General, that was the only viable option. The felines should have no option but to attack us from their position of weakness. If that did not happen, then we had to attack them from our position of strength.

The General rebutted one objection after another. He argued that it was the balance of power between the Overlords that had discouraged them from actively warring between themselves. In our case, General Jack explained there was a huge difference in power, at least in the powerful rulers' mind set.

There was no doubt in the General's mind that the enemy would consider the operation he was about to propose as an act of war. (**Page182, #7**)

The commanders shrugged their shoulders and let it pass. After the assembly when they had surrendered their vote, any innate reservations they expressed in debates were allowed to be brushed aside without much ado.

II

 In each of the three areas of operation, we again recruited the sapping animals to construct short but, deep trenches. We covered these with foliage and filled each trench with cactus trees, thorny bushes, sharp rocks and wooden pikes. In each site, a lone reindeer lured the leader of each enemy army into the trap. Representatives of our respective armies (but not the cats) quickly moved to the edges of the trap, making it a point to reveal their faces. They jeered and taunted the anguished trapped feline leaders as the monkeys gleefully pelted them. These provocative Union Jack associates challenged the trapped victims to battle, calling their rulers cowards. This latter taunt particularly stung the haughty felines. The allies then quickly withdrew and escaped before the enraged, bruised and lacerated victim could free himself from the trap.

There were no casualties on our side during these enjoyable missions. The monkeys went bananas with the excitement and joy of the venture. All in all, it was a gratifying experience for us. During these three parallel operations, it was cathartic to vent our pent-up frustrations against those tyrants, from whose immediate retaliation we were immune. Not even in my wildest dreams, did I imagine that we could pillory our Rulers with such impunity, even though it was just for a fleeting moment. It gave us an unusual feeling of empowerment.

Sabine's zest for the Union Jack's cause re-emerged when she insisted on participating in the *casus belli* missions. They were her style. She would have been in her element. We succeeded in holding her back from participating and this later proved to be providential for our battle plans.

The die was cast. The three feline groups declared war on us that same day in the three different operation zones. There was no going back now.

General Jack declared, "We have now crossed the Rubicon."

For D-Day, we had a problem. I could not scout for King Roar. Nor could Purr. We were both needed on the battlefield. But, the King expected one of our family. Sabine volunteered. Purr was reluctant to let her go. She was now pregnant with Jackat. Sabine would have had to venture behind enemy lines, straight into the heart of darkness. Purr did not want her out of his protective range. In the end, he relented. We had no choice. Sending a stranger would have raised suspicions.

III

 Poor Champ the monkey never got over his younger brother's death. He was shattered. He blamed it on General Jack and myself. From the outset, he never wanted his young brother to enrol in the mission. These missions had become too dangerous. Chimp ignored his brother's objections.

He retorted, "With General Jack and Miaow behind the operation, nothing can go wrong. They'll see to it. I'll be a hero." Since the advent of the General, it had become fashionable to be called a "hero" by taking it out on the fierce felines. Everyone dreamt of the scenario when the General would lay his hand on their right shoulder and declare him or her a hero in front of the cheering masses.

Champ unenthusiastically joined the team just to keep a watchful eye on his reckless brother.

Inside the cougar's hut, Chimp was in his element. He lost his head fooling around. Champ tried to quieten him down. He pleaded with him to make an immediate discreet exit. After all, the monkeys had completed the task. There was no point tarrying but Champ's pleas were in vain.

Chimp's mischief was fatal when he responded by loudly teasing his cautious brother. This was to attract the attention of the cougars and the rest is history.

A week before D-Day, I was at my last briefing with King Roar in his hut. A lion guard entered announcing the arrival of a monkey at the gate.

The guard added, "The monkey says he has important information for the King."

The King sneered, "What information does he have?"

The guard replied, "He spoke about hidden trench traps, about concealed snakes and about hidden taunting monkeys throwing missiles against the lions."

At the mention of trenches, monkeys and missiles, King Roar abruptly rose bristling with widened eyes, dilating pupils and flaring nostrils.

He ordered, "Bring him in. Make sure no one lays a paw on him. He must remain unharmed."

When the door opened, to my horror, my eyes locked on Champ's eyes. He was surprised to see me. He flashed a malicious smile. The look in Champ's face said, "*A life for a life. Your life for Chimp's.*" Oh no! He was about to reveal our secret battle plans. He was about to unmask my double identity. I had to escape. The King's attention was focused on Champ. Silently, I edged my way step by step to the exit. Once over the threshold, I had to dash out of the camp. It was my only chance of evading certain bloody execution. I was almost there but an agonizing shriek rattled me. I spun round to behold a disturbing sight. The King's huge mouth was open. Champ's fluttering legs protruded out of it. The floor was bloodied.

Poor Champ! My secret was safe as were our battle plans. I was safe but poor twisted Champ! Why did it have to end like that for him?

"Thou shalt not mock thy King," King Roar growled. He quoted a line from the constitution of Our Land. With a straight face, I bowed. Inside I was trembling. I was on my knees cleaning up the mess.

Shaken, I asked in a tremulous whimper, "Didn't you give orders that he was not to be touched?" I did not raise my eyes from the floor.

"Exactly!" he boomed, "I wanted him all for myself. That is how anyone who dares to challenge and taunt his or her King ends up. That will be the fate of my pathetic subjects next week. What was all that about - trenches, snakes, and the rest?"

I meekly blabbed, "He was talking about those traps they had set just before you declared war. They had set many, some of which must have been filled with snakes. You happened to fall into one that fortunately, did not have snakes. You were lucky."

He snarled and nodded. The King belched as he arrogantly slid out of the room without a word.

I discussed the incident with General Jack. He too, was sorry for Champ. The General called him the reluctant hero of the Union Jacks. Unintentionally, Champ had inadvertently saved our resistance movement on two occasions. First, when he set the stage for the rescue of my son and secondly, now when he misled King Roar on the eve of the battle. Grief had twisted Champ's mind. He must have been distraught when our rescue mission saved my son Scratchy but not his brother. Even the subsequent loss of my son did not placate his misguided thirst for revenge.

IV

 On the eve of the battle, I received the intelligence reports compiled by the sparrows about the members of the Four Kingdoms after our thwarted assassination attempt. The findings were disturbing. They revealed what would unfold after the King was deposed. The upper and middle castes of the Four Kingdoms were already jostling for dominance within their respective kingdoms. Furthermore, each of these kingdoms was already building up a rivalry with other kingdoms as to which kingdom would rule the land. Certain figures from the various animal groups were already putting themselves forward as candidates for kingship. These rivals were striving to form alliances with a view to building up their power bases. This was a chilling reminder of how hell would break loose in the aftermath of the Battle of the Five Kingdoms. Instead of one enemy, we would now be fighting countless enemy armies for the control of the land. We were on the verge of a war within a war. We were rushing headlong into anarchy.

I revealed the information to General Jack. He did not seem too surprised.

I moaned to him, "We're going through all this to rid ourselves of the dictatorship of the Feline Kingdom, only to end up with an even worse fate. We would be jumping from the frying pan of dictatorship into the fire of anarchy. Ironically, we might even become nostalgic for the days

of Feline Rule."

He replied, "Few people with leadership qualities can resist the lure of absolute power over the lives of their subjects. It will always be like that. They will always make it their life mission to achieve that power. Once they attain that power, they strive to hold on to it forever. That way, they can enjoy the fruits of that power."

"But don't worry," he continued, "We'll cross that bridge when we come to it. In the meantime, let us concentrate on next week's battle. All should fall into place with time."

"I don't know," I said.

"Have faith," he concluded, "where there's a will there's a way."

General Jack always managed to sow hope when I only saw hopelessness.

CHAPTER 9

THE BATTLE OF THE FIVE KINGDOMS

I

The fateful day arrived. As I write these words ten years after the event, my heart pounds loudly in my chest as it did then. My nerves were taut. General Jack was nervous. The gazelles were edgy. Popo the elephant was fidgety. There was heightened excitement and anxiety throughout the ranks. We had meticulously set the stage for the battle and drafted the script. Now we had to act that script. We hoped Lady Luck would look down on us favourably.

General Jack and I commanded the Army of the South. He was dressed in white and mounted a resplendent white stallion. It was an imposing sight.

We had an efficient aerial scout relay system. They kept us informed of developments on the other two battlefields. In the West, the sky was cloudless and clear blue. In the East, storm clouds were gathering. In the South, the weather was fine but it was blustery and cloudy.

The allied forces took up their positions as planned.

The scouting cats of the Union Jack were leading the unsuspecting Overlord armies to their respective battlefields. My heart raced and I broke into a cold sweat on hearing the distant but fearful war chants of the approaching feline troops. I admit I had that unpleasant gut wrenching feeling. Butterflies were let loose in my stomach, of all places. The rhythmic banging of war drums and blaring war trumpets sunk my morale further. I am but a reed in the wind. I have always been so. Valour has never been my *forte*. But, outwardly on the battlefield that day, I operated behind a façade of cool self-confidence. This did not go unnoticed by anyone. My son, Captain Purr could not take his misty, admiring eyes off me on the battlefield.

Just before they arrived, I asked General Jack a question that had been bothering me for some time.

"Why is it that at the assembly, you were reluctant to propose your plan B?"

He replied slowly, "Because you don't mess with nature. Nature cannot destroy itself. Just as the Overlords can't destroy you, we can't destroy them. I think we are destined to live side by side."

He then gazed at the chickens who were joyfully counting the increased number of eggs they expected to hatch in the absence of harsh Overlord rule.

General Jack added, "I'll believe in this victory when I see it."

The enemy arrived on the battlefields and took up the positions we envisaged.

The stage was set for the battle to commence.

Horror of horrors! It was an unmitigated disaster. Nothing went right on the day!

II

THE BATTLE OF THE WEST

The tiger army arrived on the battlefield. They studied their opponents with perplexity. The tigers were confounded. They were at a loss on how to proceed. They dilly-dallied over drawing first blood. Which army would launch the opening attack? In the end, the out-of-sorts tiger army opted on the side of caution. The initiative for attack therefore rested with the elephant army. For that, they had to await the Signal in the Sky.

The leaf-bearing dove was due to be released in three hours' time. The tigers were still in a state of shock. They had been on tenterhooks since they arrived on the battlefield in a bullish mood. The felines were not permitted sufficient time to calm their jittery

nerves; because another curious leafless white dove flew by three hours before the expected launch time. Popo the excitable elephant chief inexplicably mistook the intruder as the Signal in the Sky. At Popo's screeching command, the entire mass of shrieking elephants poured over the hill into the path of the opposing tiger army. They kicked up a massive cloud of dust in their wake. The ground shook. In the face of this unexpected oncoming *force majeure*, the already distressed tigers panicked. They broke ranks and fled eastward. The elephants chased them. In that instant, *the two opposing Western armies became the Eastern Train.*

Figure 4: The Battle of the West

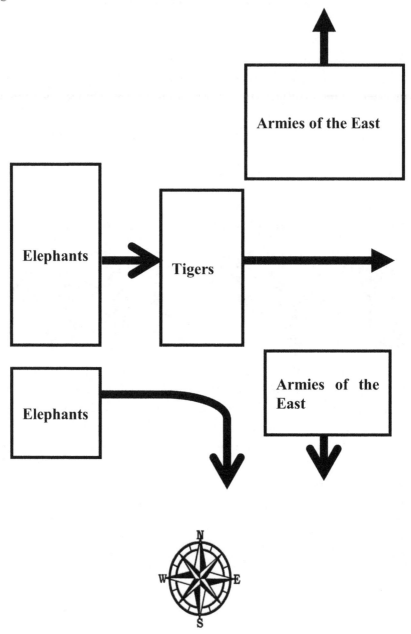

There followed a mad uninterrupted eastward run overshadowed above by the mystified scouting squadron of crows. After a three-hour dash covering thousands of miles, they entered the Eastern battleground!

First, the waiting armies that had already been arrayed on the Eastern Battleground heard the distant rumble. Next, they caught a glimpse on the western horizon of the dust cloud topped by the black cloud of crows. Then, the stampede came in focus. Seeing the stampede gaining ground on them, the Armies of the East (both allied and Overlord) had just enough time to split in two. They created a wide passage for the Eastern Train to pass through. **(Page182, #6)** One half of both allied and enemy armies moved northward. The other half of each army was displaced southward. Even the dense cloud of scouting eagles of the Eastern Army had to split. That way they created a passage in the sky for the crows of the Eastern Train to pass through.

The approaching elephant stampede was too wide to pass through the passage created, so one third of the southern elephant flank veered southwards at a right angle. This alarmed detachment of elephants did not stop running in the new direction.

The opposing Armies of the East stood rooted to the ground dumbfounded as they gaped through the haze at the passing Eastern Train. They were stuck in the mud, engulfed in a massive mushroom-shaped dust cloud. When the dust finally cleared, they could make out the distant lumbering Eastern Train finally receding as a puff of dust on the eastern horizon.

III

THE BATTLE OF THE EAST

A flash storm broke out an hour before the planned signal for battle. It rained cats and dogs. I have already related how the Eastern Train had bisected the battleground in a thunderous rampage. This was unforeseen.

The displaced armies (both allied and Overlord) were unnerved and disoriented because of both the improbable stampede and the violent flash thunderstorm. Razor-sharp tension was in the air. It gripped the opposing armies.

An exceptionally loud thunderclap rattled the ground. The animals felt it in their bones. A particularly powerful streak of lightning further startled the restless animals. There had been a brief, transient lull in the downpour.

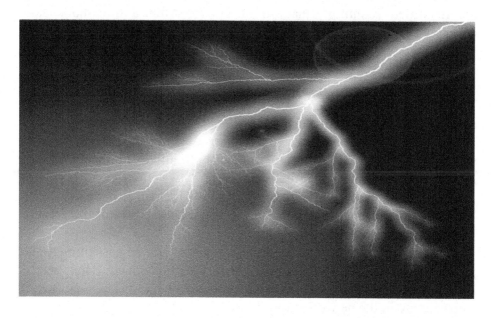

It so happened that a tree struck by lightning just in front of the allied heavy cavalry caught fire. This small blaze triggered off an untimely stampede of the frightened heavy cavalry (led by the bison and buffalo). The problem was, the charge was in the *wrong* direction!

They stampeded westward in the direction of their light shock cavalry colleagues amassed behind them. The heavy cavalry unit was meant to charge *eastward* in the direction of the enemy, *not* westward! When the stationary light cavalry division saw their heavy cavalry colleagues closing down on them, they had no choice. Led by the wolves, they ran for their lives. They too, burst forth *westward* with the frightened heavy cavalry trailing.

On witnessing this reverse charge, the southern lancer flank (led by the reindeer) interpreted this as a signal for a concerted retreat. They *too* stampeded westward!

Figure 5: The Battle of the East (first phase)

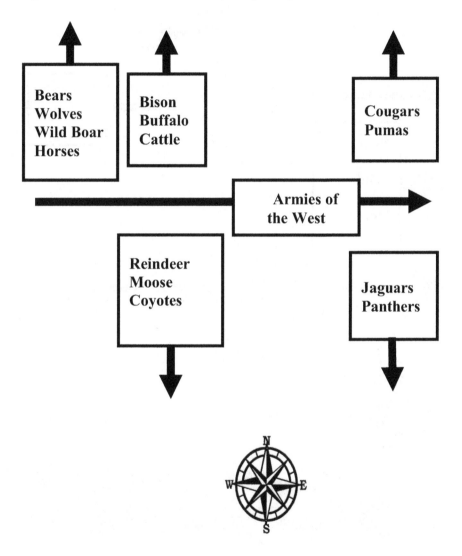

Figure 6: The Battle of the East (second phase)

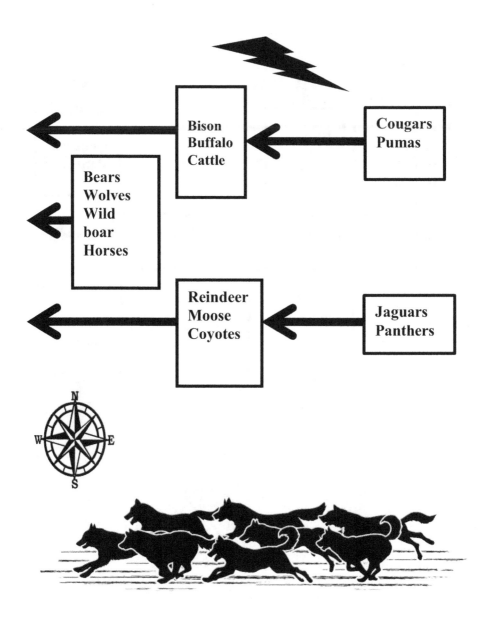

Together these three divisions formed the vanguard of the newly created Western Train! This unplanned flight prompted the cougars, pumas, panthers and jaguars to take advantage of the enemy's flight and attack. The pursuit by the felines completed the rear part of the train. Earlier on, the feline army was disturbed and irritable because of the unforeseen succession of disturbing events. Once the allied army bolted, the felines smelt blood. They gave in to their bloodlust and exploded from the blocks in tempestuous style.

The call of the prey was irresistible. The felines pursued the prey relentlessly. In that bizarre manner, the Western Train rolled westward followed by the overhead eagle scouts. The sound of the thunderous stampede complemented the crashing sound of thunder. Streaks of lightning in the leaden sky under the sleeting rain lit up the awesome scene of the Western Train's departure from the battleground.

IV

THE BATTLE OF THE SOUTH

 The lions and their cousins arrived on the battlefield as forecasted. They were startled by the size of the allied forces. **(Page183,#12)** If the arrogant lions were amazed by what they saw, they would have been staggered by the presence of the lined-up troops concealed in the forest and in the trenches. They were to be shocked and awed by what followed. For starters, they caught sight of the impressive figure of General Jack mounted on his steed. The white stallion cantered elegantly back and forth while the General imperviously surveyed the battlefield. The bright morning sun had just emerged from behind a cloud. It illuminated the magnificent scene. The brilliant white radiance of General Jack and his stallion was arresting. It upped the ante somehow. It enlightened and inflamed his fainthearted troops. King Roar caught sight of this ethereal figure. He squinted his eyes against the light and grimaced. He did not know what to make of it. For once, he was befuddled and he stared at the General blankly. I had never seen him look so stupid before.

To say he was awestruck was an understatement. The clash between General Jack and King Roar was about to unfold in a daunting encounter. I was proud to stand at the General's feet, the whiteness of my cat blended in well with his whiteness. We were as one. It was a spine tingling experience. His radiance engulfed me. My son Purr said I sparkled that day.

About half an hour before the Signal in the Sky was due, General Jack gave a signal. Hell was unleashed in every sense of the word. The long-range artillery bombardment against the enemy lines commenced. It was devastating. The monkeys hurled beehives (the bees, wasps and hornets had consented. They had a whale of a time stinging the enemy). The artillery monkeys also hurled decomposing carcasses, stones, tree trunks, cactus trees, bones and coconuts. Some of the coconuts launched were solid. Others had their tips cut off. The monkeys filled the hollow shells with stones or poisonous scorpions.**(Page183,#11)** We called them scorpion bombs. The missiles rained down incessantly on the jumpy felines.

The felines lashed out at the stinging, buzzing bugs to no avail. They slashed the thin air, they slashed themselves, they mutilated themselves and their neighbours in the process. The scorpions' poisonous stings were hallucinogenic. The missiles transmuted into oncoming flying demons, their feline neighbours transmogrified into ogres. They became hairy, scary, quite contrary monsters. We watched in amazement as the stung felines frantically lashed out at each other. The feline army was tearing itself apart. It was caught in a maelstrom of ghouls, fiends and spectres. King Roar looked askance first in our direction and then at his army. On one side, he heard the cheers and jeers. On the other, he heard the agonizing howls of his troops. He could not come to terms with the implausibility of his fearless felines reduced to that pitiable state. Truly, it was a surreal moment. The King was hesitant. Was he losing his mettle?

During the bombardment, a large group of excited mice ran forward in the forest to occupy the front seats. They were determined to have a good view of the hilarious spectacle. It was not often that lions were roughened up in that droll manner. The rodents' presence unnerved the concealed elephants, who in turn unnerved the rhinos and hippos. *Oh no!* An untimely wayward stampede was in the making. When the mice realised, they swiftly retreated to the back seats. They did not want to upset the battle plans. Fortunately, the elite heavy troops calmed down. The spectacle of the harassed, discomforted lions had a comforting and satisfying effect on their nerves.

The tide of battle was in our favour.

A gust of wind arose out of the blue. It dislodged the colourful standard, carrying it away. It fluttered in the wind but then settled on a southern treetop when the wind suddenly died down. The allies were about to construct another flag to mark the direction for the simulated retreat of the light cavalry. However, there was no time for it. The lions' endurance was reaching its limit. Submerged under the sunlight-blocking shower of endless missiles, they were at the mercy of the stinging wasps and scorpions. They were dazed and confused. The turmoil in the felines' ranks was breath taking as they were swamped by a black cloud of stinging, grotesque demons. The felines were at the end of their tether. Was King Roar wavering?

The sheer scale of what was unfolding around the King was overwhelming. The battle was all but won for us. A decisive victory was there for the taking. It was a battle of wills between the two leaders. The General was resolute, the fate of the animal world was in the balance. The stakes would never be so high in animal history. General Jack feared the fierce felines were about to flee. A mass retreat of the feline army would have robbed us of the ultimate victory. The consequences would have been tragic for us. Undoubtedly, the felines would regroup after a few days and mercilessly overrun us in no time at all. Our cause would thus be lost forever. The hard won element of surprise had been our only formidable war asset. Having now forfeited the weaponized surprise element, we would be in no position to mount any resistance. We would become grist for the mill in the ensuing widespread slaughter. The moment was auspicious. This time, there were no two ways around it, the General could not delay anymore. So, he took the fateful decision prematurely.

General Jack gave the signal ten minutes before it was due - we released the dove bearing the reddish green leaf. The gazelles noted the signal and commenced their flight... in the *wrong* direction! They flew *southward* in the direction of the entrapped standard, *not* in the westward direction of the trenches. This sparked off a furious charge by the long-suffering lions, cheetahs and leopards. The crazed feline attack in turn, was the signal for the pre-planned intimidating, thunderous charge by the elephants, rhinos and hippos of the forest. In this manner, the Southern Train took shape followed by the overhead falcon scouts. *The elite divisions of the Army of the South and the feline army became the Southern Train.* The Southern Train hurtled along southward in the direction of the Great White Ice Lake and departed from the Southern Battleground. **(Page182,#4)** The remainder of our army stood by speechless and incredulous. All heads were turned southward in unison.

Figure 7: The Battle of the South

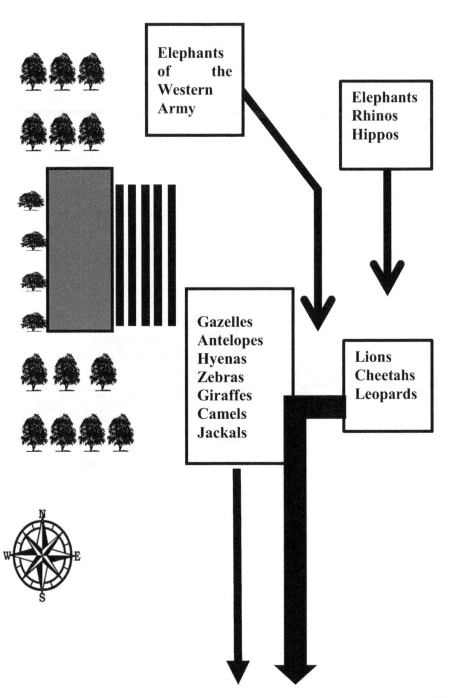

Then, phenomena elsewhere grabbed our attention. The ground quaked. Our ears turned in the direction of a rumble from the north. We scanned the northern horizon and made out a mysterious moving cloud in the distance. We did not know what it was.

Our faces were simultaneously directed northward. We finally beheld the incredible sight of a large wildly stampeding elephant division! What kind of cosmic riddle was this?

We gawked at the frenzied elephants as they stormed past. The ground under our feet trembled. Our line of vision vibrated, the trees rattled. Their screeching was deafening. The end of the world was nigh! A cloud of dust engulfed us. After recovering from a long drawn out coughing fit, we all strained our eyes and surveyed the southern horizon through the dusty mist. The rumble became fainter and the fleeing dust cloud eventually merged with the cloud of the Southern Train. The stomping elephants that appeared out of thin air had finally caught up with the other fleeing armies that galloped ahead of them. In that manner, another - a fourth compartment - was added to the growing Southern Train. What sorcery was at play here? How did these elephants appear out of nowhere? At the time, we did not know it but *this was the remnant of the Western Army that had bizarrely traversed three battlegrounds!*

Our eyes were compulsively fixed on the southern horizon until the cloud of dust faded. We stalled in a state of shock. There was dead silence. Rather we were temporarily tone deaf after that ear shattering din. Our ears would not stop ringing. Everyone held his or her breath. Some wide-eyed animals blinked, others scratched their heads and others rubbed their eyes in disbelief.

More was to come. We were in for another surprise.

Upheaval in the trenches attracted our collective spaced-out attention. Just at our feet we were about to witness an incredible battle within a battle.

V

THE BATTLE OF THE SNAKES

 The snakes were furious. They had just been cheated of their intended prey. The enraged snakes turned on themselves in frustration. They hissed, they squirmed, they grappled and they bit. A diabolical battle ebbed and flowed. After about half an hour of futile conflict, the pythons had had enough. They spat their scorn and fled southward *en masse* chasing their intended original prey - the lions. These pythons formed the final compartment of the Southern Train.

Our collective line of vision instinctively flitted back and forth between the trenches and the southern horizon until the pythons disappeared.

Something else caught our attention in the trenches. Disgusted because of the stalemate inside the trenches, the remaining snakes emerged without warning. They fled in directions as far away from each other as possible. The rattlesnakes surged westward in search of the cougars, pumas, panthers and jaguars. They formed the fifth compartment of the Western Train! The Cobras bustled eastward following the path of the tigers thereby forming the third compartment of the Eastern Train! The disgruntled vipers scrambled northward into no animal's land! They receded from our sight, thankfully.

We lingered on in disbelief. We stood stunned, speechless and motionless for over an hour. We stared into space, contemplating these events. Each one of us tried unsuccessfully to take in all that had just unfolded before our tired eyes.

It was staggering. Surely, the battlefield was haunted.

CHAPTER 10

THE AFTERMATH

I

By then we had received the reports from the scouts of the other two battlefields. It was nothing but a complete collapse of our battle plans. Not a single skirmish had occurred! Not a single casualty! Not one! After all those preparations, it was a bitter pill to swallow. **(Page183,#8)**We failed! We had lost the battle! It was infuriating.

Our entire resistance was a protracted cloak and dagger operation. We had just about succeeded in the cloak stage, but we failed spectacularly at the dagger stage. We could not deliver the *coup de grâce* and do away with Feline Rule once and for all. Throughout, absolute secrecy had been the key to our success. We had gone through great lengths to maintain our mission's secrecy. We had now unmasked ourselves during the battle in a one-time, life-or-death gamble. But, we had carelessly forfeited the element of surprise for good. Now, we were exposed and vulnerable. Our cause was lost forever, we had no future. We had it in our paws but we had thrown it away!

How was it possible? What had we done to deserve this debacle? The high water mark was the battering of the felines by the giggling monkeys and their simian cousins. Victory was within our grasp. Then, it cruelly eluded us. All because of a mistake by our supposedly elite elephant troops. A single, simple mistake had triggered off a cascading avalanche of unfortunate events! Everyone was jittery on D-Day, but that was no excuse for the bungling on the battlefields.

The pompous, pot-bellied elephant commander Popo had bragged before the battle.

"Leave it to me. Do not worry. Everything will go like clockwork. Take it from me. Consider it done," he said.

Did those accursed elephants need to go on a mad rampage across the land? They messed up not one but three battlefields. Whatever

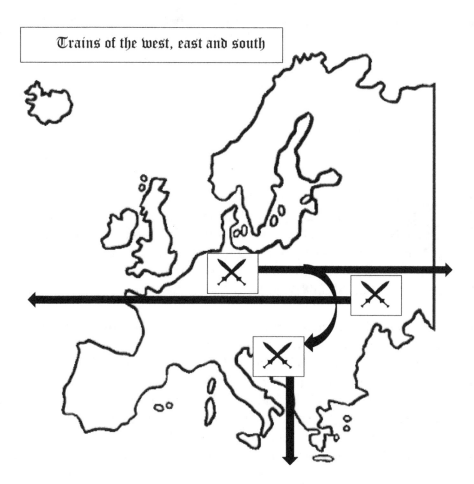

possessed those beserkers to run amok? What evil spirit was at work here? The elephants fluffed it badly. They threw everyone off, both friend and foe.

Many years later I realised that a dove with or without a big green leaf looked identical to an elephant. Elephants are colour blind. Hence the bizarre misreading of the battle signal on the battlefield.

We also paid a heavy price for not having a substitute standard to guide the gazelle-led charge. Again, one tiny oversight cascaded into a torrential sequence of damning errors.

Then there were those feckless gazelles. After all those drills, they could not tell left from right, north from south.

Sprite the gazelle commander of the light cavalry had boasted,

"We will gracefully lead the charge of the light brigade into the trenches of death."

Some charge they led! Away from the trenches of death!

Besides, there was that misdirected bull run that messed up the Eastern Battleground. They panicked when they saw the red blaze. Ordinarily, raging bulls charge into the enemy, but it had to be an innocuous natural event to frighten those worthless bulls. The fierce felines had nothing to do with the rout.

These fools were no longer with us. How I would have blasted them if they were. I fumed all day long, I was in a foul mood for months.

Moreover, there were those despicable snakes. I could never get myself to approach them. General Jack somehow seduced them into our ranks. He did so by blowing music on his short bamboo stick. He referred to the snake division as his secret weapon, he was proud of them. Myself, I saw a depressing foreshadowing of the anarchy that would have ensued had we won the Battle of the Five Kingdoms. General Jack must have been a genius to place the snake division in front of us. Had they been behind us, they would have undoubtedly stabbed us in the back.

I found some kind of comfort in these recriminations.

There was one bright spot in this damned affair. It was Sabine, that plucky, adopted daughter of mine I was so fond of. General Jack used to call her "Thunder Heart" and so it was. She related that the King was so desperately impatient to reach the battleground, he would have arrived at least three hours before the appointed time. That would have upset all our plans on the Southern Battleground.

I asked her, "So how did you delay them?"

"Oh, it was simple, Papi. I told them there was a magic potion which deadened their pain, which would make them more aggressive and which would raise their fighting spirits."

"What did King Roar say?"

"He said, 'Oh! Ah! Really? Give it to us then. I order you.'

"I replied, 'The problem, Your Majesty, is that these poppies lie in fields about three hours' walk yonder. We will arrive on the battlefield at least three hours late.'

"The King said, 'Huh! Silence! You stupid scum of a cat. You don't tell me what to do. We shall march forth. On to those poppy fields we go. Then, we march into battle.'

"I took them there after a few intentional time-wasting mini-detours. I told the King I was not entirely sure of the location. I innocently fluttered my eyelids at him as I looked him in his all-seeing eye. He believed me. He said, 'Huh? You move on, you stupid cat!' When we arrived, the lions

devoured the opium. One fourth of the army was not in fighting condition, even though they thought otherwise. It's a pity there wasn't enough for the entire army."

"How did you know of the fields?"

" I didn't know those poppy fields existed. Twinkle had told me about them. She had sent me off to collect some for Scratchy, when he was fatally injured."

"You minx!" I laughed. Oh yes! Sabine was resourceful and she was shrewd. She had gone into the lion's den, led the great King himself out of it by the nose, and taken him on a wild goose hunt. No one had ever outfoxed the King before in that manner.

"Now, why didn't *we* think about that ourselves before? It was a typical Scratchy move. He would have been proud of his *protégé*. We should have had you in the high command," I enthused. The pregnant Sabine had delightfully tricked the most powerful army ever. It was spilt milk, though, and I could not even lap it up.

General Jack was broken, crestfallen and deflated but he rallied quickly.

II

"The Feline Overlords will soon return in a few days' time," General Jack remarked. "There'd be hell to pay, especially for the newly exposed treacherous cats of the Union Jack. It's imperative that all the troops scatter and go into hiding until the Overlords' ire cools down."

Our massive army, still reeling from the defeat, broke up. Animals scurried into hiding. Here, there, everywhere. A sense of impending doom pervaded the air. We expected the worst. No one had ever challenged the feline authority and lived. **(Page185,#5)**That was the curse of Our Land.

On his part, the General planned to escape over the mountains into the Dark Land. He would seek out a safe place for us to settle. Afterwards, he would return to lead us into exile. I insisted on going with him. He said he was leaving at noon the next day, but he wanted me to stay.

"Look around you," he said, "what do you see? Chickens, donkeys, sheep, goats, rabbits… They need a cool head to guide them into safety. You will be more useful here."

I resolved to follow the General, I had already made the arrangements. I appointed my trusted son, Captain Purr to assume overall command of the resistance movement. I told the General, "Look, I'm coming with you, whether you like it or not. I'll be there at noon."

He looked me in the eye for a few seconds. He tapped me on the back and wagged a cautionary finger at me, saying, "Remember Miaow. Whatever happens, always keep the faith," and he walked away.

The next day at noon, I went to our meeting place at the iconic W-shaped tree. General Jack was not there. I waited an hour. Smug-faced, George the fox approached me, never taking his penetrating gaze off me during his short walk.

"I saw the General depart at first light in the direction of the mountains," he sneered.

I did not swoon. My heart sank and I gasped. For a few seconds, the news paralysed my mind. In front of me, George became blurred. The revelation bowled me over. When I finally unwound, I took leave of George. Without looking at him, I said dryly, "Thanks for letting me know, George. I'll be on my way now."

"Are you sure you're alright?"

I gave the sarcastic fox a casual wave and I slouched off. George the fox did not move. He did not take his cold eyes off me as I walked away. Throughout my walk, I felt George's sinister eyes fixed on my back. I was discomforted by his stern, pensive gaze. It never wavered for one instant. My silhouette finally disappeared from his line of vision. Only then did he move on.

I pulled myself together and thought about the implications. Though bitterly disappointed, I realised it was for the better. I had responsibilities and duties that I had to attend to, here. Because of my senior position, I was the best animal to deal with them. I only regretted that I could not bid the General farewell. At least, I had the consolation of his promise to return. I knew that General Jack always kept his promises.

"Keep the faith". Those were his last words. I kept them in my heart.

CHAPTER 11

THE RECKONING

The days turned to weeks, the weeks turned to months, but there still was no sign of General Jack. I developed the habit of looking to the eastern mountains expecting him to present himself as he did on the first day.

It was also odd that our Overlords had not yet returned.

I

THE EASTERN TRAIL

After six months, I received a strange report from the scouting crows of the Eastern Train. The train did not stop running. The runners had no respite. They covered millions of miles and faltered only when they reached the Far Eastern coastline of the Dark Land. Exhausted, the elephants, the tigers and the cobras settled in different parts of the land.

To my surprise, the chief crow told me that the land is not dark. On the contrary, it is colourful, with yellow areas, green areas, brown areas and white areas.

I did not dwell much on the information the crows gave me up to that point.

But then, the crow also told me that he saw many erect two-legged creatures migrating westward. These were bigger versions of General Jack. This piece of news alarmed me. The habitual fear of the unknown preoccupied me. What threat will these migratory creatures bring with them? As usual, I was in two minds about the entire situation. I was uncomfortable that their arrival might possibly add to the dire uncertainty of these times. On the other hand, I was content, because it meant that General Jack was on his way back.

Figure 8: The Eastern Train

II

THE SOUTHERN TRAIL

Three month later, the scouting falcons of the Southern Train arrived. They gave me their bewildering account.

"The cumbersome Southern Train was relentless in its run. The terrified gazelles /antelopes/zebras/giraffes/camels/hyenas/jackals led the run. These were hounded by the lions/cheetahs/leopards.

"The felines in the front part of their compartment were ferociously snapping at the heels of the pacesetting enemies. The felines in the middle hurtled on in a bewildered, intoxicated state consequent on the intense artillery bombardment they had been subjected to. The felines at the rear of the compartment were terrified, constantly glancing backwards at their stalkers in the following compartments

. Their stalkers were two huge stamping regiments-the elephants/rhinos/hippos of the Southern Army, followed by the hopelessly disoriented elephant remnant division of the Western Army. A long sliver of raving pythons trailed them. These loathsome creatures struggled, but always managed to keep up with the pack until the end of the months' long run.

"Then, a wondrous thing happened. As the Southern Train plodded over the slippery Great White Ice Lake, its tremendous vibrations split the ice. The cracks became progressively longer, wider and more numerous. The Ice Lake broke up everywhere in the wake of the train's chaotic passage."

Falco the chief falcon scout interjected, "You see Miaow, the Southern Train rudely woke up the Spirit of the Great White Ice Lake. Furious at having his peace disturbed so brazenly, the Great Water Spirit arose to swallow up the violators. The water furies the Spirit despatched after the Southern Train, almost but not quite, managed to reach it. At all times, the train was one short step ahead. The endless sprint was a grim race against death by drowning. The name I gave this angry  giant wave was tsunami. I have never seen anything like it.

"The tsunami inexorably chased the bewildered train for many, many miles until the animals reached safety in the dry land. During its course, this colossal tsunami became bigger and bigger, wider and wider. Wherever it flowed, the Great White Ice Lake ceased to exist. Instead, it was replaced by very high levels of water that almost reached us falcons in our flight. We had just witnessed the Great Deluge. It was nothing but the tears of the Great Water Spirit. You must understand Miaow, he wept a great sea of tears when his water furies failed to catch the runaway train."

Figure 9: The Southern Train

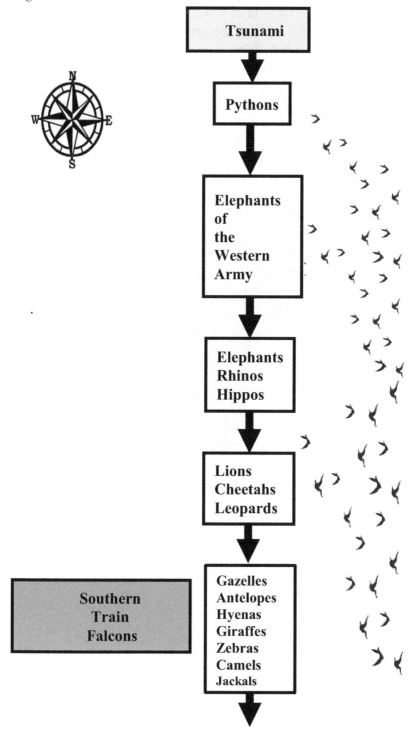

131

"The Southern Train finally reached the dry land. One half of the land was yellow and the other lower half was green. The yellow part was too dry and hot. I didn't even see a drop of water there. So the Southern Train had to continue running until it found the green land. The only exception was the camel division which had had enough of this mad running. The camels were happy to drop out of the runaway train and remain in the yellow land.

"When the rest of the train arrived in the green land, they were too exhausted to fight anymore. The various divisions went off in different directions and henceforth they settled in the New Land."

This news took me by surprise. It was so unexpected. Boy, did I need this happy news! That meant that the lions, cheetahs and leopards could not return to Our Land even if they wanted to. The miracle of the Great White Ice Lake had seen to it. Their fate was thus sealed forever.

III

THE WESTERN TRAIL

 Three months later, the Eagle Scout Division of the Western Train returned with an even crazier account.

The Western Train continued its clumsy trek even on the slippery surface of the Great White Ice Lake for miles and miles. In the vanguard, there were the bears/horses/wild boar/wolves.

The bison/buffalo/cattle/reindeer/moose/coyotes followed these. Hot on their heels, were the cougars/jaguars/panthers.

The rattlesnakes were not far behind. They doggedly gave chase to the fleeing felines. Here as well, the seismic vibrations of this huge train split the Great White Ice Lake as the crazy train rumbled on. A massive tsunami arose that was on the verge of engulfing the entire Western Train. All members of the train were petrified. The Great White Ice Lake was gradually replaced by high-level water as far as the eagle eye could see. The process of ice breakage was progressive. The running was frantic and relentless. The runners were running for their lives, fleeing the watery jaws of death. There was no slackening of pace. That would have been tantamount to mass extinction. It was a wonder the runners' lungs did not reach bursting point. They had to dig deep into their vital reserves of stamina to survive.

The disorderly Western Train finally reached the dry land in the Far West on the other side of the Great White Lake after months of non-stop running. All the runners, except the jaguars and panthers were dead tired. They collapsed motionless on the land.

The upper half of this new land was white and the lower half was green.

Glider, the chief of the eagles then continued, "Out of nowhere appeared these amazing hordes of giant green beasts. When they ran, the earth shook. We called them Dyna-Roars. They were bigger, louder and more dynamic versions of King Roar.

"When the resting panting animals saw them approaching, the thunderstruck panthers and jaguars still had some wind left in them. They startled and took off south. All the other members of the train lay prostrate and unresponsive. These didn't have the energy to be startled let alone thunderstruck by the monstrous apparitions. *Will this nightmare never end?*

"The Dyna-Roars ignored the washed out non-felines and the cougars. They sidestepped them thinking they were dead. These green monsters unleashed an incredibly fierce hunt for the two fleeing Feline Overlord divisions. Each Dyna-Roar had the combined strength of ten thousand King Roars and a 100,000 times more of his energy. One Dyna-Roar was a million times louder than King Roar. It gladdened my heart to see these felines finally getting a taste of their own medicine. You know Miaow, when I remember what your two sisters and many others went through, I considered this to be poetic justice. At times though, I must confess, I almost felt sorry for these frightened felines.

134

"From the skies, I had seen many grim death runs under the cruel Feline Rule, but this never-ending death race was apocalyptic.

"The chase occurred on the coastline. Under the crushing weight of the vast, cumbersome army of thumping Dyna-Roars, the coast started breaking up. It was an explosive scene, as one explosion followed another throughout the southern run. The Dyna-Roars fell into the rapidly rising waters. The further south the Dyna-Roars ran, the more they perished in the sea. More and more Dyna-Roars joined the southbound chase of what remained of the Western Train. Strangely, *the previous Western train had now become the Southern Train* composed of terrified jaguars/panthers and Dyna-Roars, with us eagles on top. The Western Train had previously been chased by a deadly, watery giant wave; the Southern Train was now chased by a successive wave of interminable explosions. At least, that's what it looked like from the skies above. Rubble, trees, sea spray and debris was flying off at all angles. There was this ever-lengthening massive cloud of dust and smog in the explosive wake of the Dyna-Roars' thunderous trail.

"The new Southern Train arrived at a long narrow bridge connecting the northern land with an even greener large southern land. As the awesome Dyna-Roars charged madly, more and more of this bridge broke up under their combined weight. The bridge became narrower and narrower. Eventually, it became too narrow for the Dyna-Roars. Not one made it to the southern land. All the others drowned. These monsters had brought about their own destruction. At last, the winded jaguars and panthers

 rested. They flopped onto the ground and lay prone for many days. They could not believe what they had just been through. Of all the members of the Western Train, they had covered most ground. In due course, they settled in different parts of that land which they colonised.

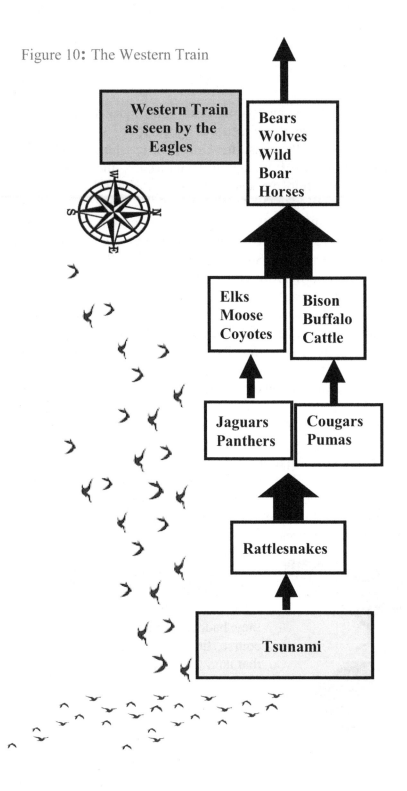

Figure 10: The Western Train

Western Train as seen by the Eagles

Bears Wolves Wild Boar Horses

Elks Moose Coyotes

Bison Buffalo Cattle

Jaguars Panthers

Cougars Pumas

Rattlesnakes

Tsunami

"On our return journey we were in for another surprise. The Great White Ice Lake was replaced by water throughout. I don't know where all this water came from, but my flight companions were convinced that the profuse perspiration of the runners had created an ocean of salty sweat. We were even more surprised to see animals in it with no arms and legs, nor hair or feathers. They had different shapes and sizes. It was all very fishy so we called them fish. We tried to befriend them. As we hovered just above the water level, we called out to them but they did not understand our language."

Glider said, "In fact, some of them were rude to us. There were these  massive fish the size of a mountain. Actually, they looked more like swimming volcanoes because they had a hole in the summit. I descended on the edge of a hole in the roof of one of them.

"I shouted, 'Hello! My name is Glider! Who are you? What is your name?' into this strange mouth since most of his body was under the water. I don't know how he heard me because I could not see any ears. Maybe they were under the water. But hear me he did, because you know how he responded, Miaow?

"He spat a huge, powerful jet of water that threw me up into the sky. I was fortunate this animal was a water dragon not a fire dragon. He would have otherwise roasted me alive. This must have been some kind of war signal, because his companions promptly shot water jets at us. So we took flight. We steered clear of these moving volcanoes during the rest of our odyssey. You couldn't be sure if they'd spew water or fire from their mouths.

"One day in the middle of the Great Lake, I saw a small rock. I was tired so I went to rest on it. This immediately activated an inner mechanism inside the rock. A strange head popped out together with four legs. These legs paddled. The unsteadiness of the rock threw me into the deep freezing water. I even caught a cold afterwards. Damn it! We saw many of these moving rocks. You can't rest on them. You'll end up with the sniffles.

"On another day, I saw a large fish just below the surface with a triangular arm cutting through the water. His arm was pointing towards me. He must have been offering me a lift. I was tired. I appreciated the kind offer to rest and to cover sea miles at the same time.

So, I rested on his offered arm. It was so sharp; it cut through my claws. It's sharper than a lion's fangs. 'No thank you,' I told him and I took off."

Glider continued, "On another day, we saw some objects moving fast just below the surface. We flew low to investigate. They were even fishier fish. These big fish had flippers and they had a long beak. They screamed at us. They jumped up at us. They were aggressively fishing for us. They were fiercely defending their water territory from us. We had to escape before they fished us out of the sky. If we didn't fly away, there were so many of them, we would have been fished out of existence. Miaow, I have reached the conclusion that these fish are no different to the lions. They are just as fierce and uncompromising. We must stay away from them. Take it from me, I who have seen all the wonders of the world."

Strange days, I mused. Strange days indeed!

The events of the three battlefields were more earth shattering than we had thought.

IV

Glider went on and on. I had become joyfully distant by then. I heard him say something about why he had named the northern land the Wild West. It was because of all the wild happenings he had witnessed there. From then on it remained known as the "Wild West". Glider raved about how the jaguars had survived not only a *deus ex machina* annihilation, but also the demonic rage of those other worldly green monsters. Since these intrepid feline warriors were now dominant in the southern land, he named this territory, "The Land of the Jaguar" because they were the first to arrive in the new land. They had outrun the panthers. Glider was in a self-congratulatory mood. He waxed lyrical on why he was the world's first explorer. He boasted he had seen things nobody else had seen. He bragged that he had boldly gone where no animal had gone before. He had charted new territories. He puffed up his chest, spread his wings and loudly proclaimed the Great Glider Trail. He said he would start an airfreight transportation service. Because of their strong claws, his eagle squadron could transport any animal (below a certain weight) to the New Lands against weight-adjusted payment, of course. He proudly asserted he was the Father of the New Lands. Henceforth, it was known as *Terra Nova*, though the eagles insisted on calling it Glider's Land. I did not care about what he saw or did not see. I was not interested in the names of the land. Glider's self-praise did not turn me on. The only news that excited me was the realisation that we were now free from those wild animals, be they friend or foe.

Listening to the account, I stood trembling with emotion. My heart fluttered. My peel bristled. My eyes welled up.

The news inflated me until I finally exploded, "We won! We won! He was right! General Jack was right! He was right in everything! Victory! Victory! He was right all along! The land is ours! They can never come back! We are free! Free! We won after all!"

I repeated this litany endlessly. I danced around like a mad cat. The news had released the lifelong bottled-up tension in this one memorable day. The triumphant message spread like wildfire all through the land. The wild celebrations continued for many weeks. There were more casualties in the celebrations than in the crazy Battle of the Five Kingdoms!

I overflowed with joy. I was joyful for my family. I felt joy for both General Jack and myself. We had been vindicated and Scratchy had not died in vain, after all.

Having recovered from this pleasant shock, I quickly summoned as many birds as possible to scour Our Land and the Dark Land. Their mission was to seek General Jack. We had to break the good news and tell him to return as soon as possible. He still considered himself a loser and a fugitive. I spent as much time as possible at the W-shaped tree. I insisted on being the first animal to greet him privately and welcome him in this free land. I was in a jubilant mood for many weeks.

Us two, more than anyone else, knew the significance of this victory. For us it was a double victory. Firstly, we had managed to overthrow the Feline Kingdom forever. Secondly, and even more importantly, we had averted the inevitably interminable anarchic battles. We had unexpectedly achieved this through the permanent banishment of the aggressively powerful upper and middle classes of the other kingdoms. We secured this dual victory by conducting a peculiar battle. It was a battle that was never fought. Inexplicable water magic did the rest. As an additional bonus (for me at least), we rid ourselves of those odious venomous snakes.

All this called for a celebration! I coveted the moment. I needed to share this exhilarating experience with my closest friend. We had conquered the old world. Together, we had a bright future. It was a gratifying feeling.

It had rained all day. The grey clouds finally dispersed and the rain abated. The sun broke through. A wonderful double rainbow made its appearance in the crisp blue sky. It heralded a new age. A bright new world was opening up to us.

CHAPTER 12

THE NEW WORLD

I

The months passed by. There was no sign of General Jack. I sent wave after wave of flying scouts but it was futile. After three more years of flying, the scouts refused to fly any more of these missions. How dared they refuse? Did they not know I could have struck them down for their impudence? Whatever stopped me from wringing their impertinent necks?

Day after day, I waited for the General in our meeting place. I became more and more irascible.

I struggled to adapt to the reality of the new world. I was out of my depth.

One day, PikPak the leader of the chickens accosted me with his delegation.

"Whatever has gone wrong? We had anticipated that we would each be producing twelve eggs a week. Now, we're only producing one or two eggs a week. Why is that?"

I stifled a yawn.

"I have no idea."

"But you must know. You can fix it for us. You're the Magician of the Five Kingdoms."

"Am I? I'm sorry. I can't help. You have to sort it out yourselves."

"Bah! We were better off under Feline Rule. At least then, we each produced six eggs a week. Our economy performed better in those days."

Another day, Buffy the leader of the rabbits waylaid me

"Miaow, we can't get any rest. The birds sing all night. They sing ballads about you and the Battle of the Five Kingdoms. What then, with those silly cockerels that have now started to crow all night? They never did that before. The dogs can't sleep as well. They bark madly like there's no tomorrow. They bark at the moon. They too, join in the loud chorus of the ghost moon orchestra. Please stop them, we can't take it anymore."

"Why should I? What is it to me? Let them sing and bark if they want to." All the while, I scrutinized a fascinating tree over his shoulder.

"But, but… under Feline Rule, we slept in peace. The nights were peaceful at least. We were better off then. There wasn't all this noise."

On another day, Harold the chief of the goats complained.

"Miaow, we can't even get to the stream to drink. The horses get there first and they spend ages washing themselves. The donkeys stay there all day and they won't budge. Then the sheep arrive and they block access to the stream, It's impossible to drink or wash. By the time the others leave, the water is filthy. Please do something about it, Miaow."

"What do you want me to do?"

"Well, you're the victor of the Battle of the Five Kingdoms. If you overthrew the Five Kingdoms, you can easily clear the crowds at the stream. You can do anything."

"That, I cannot do, I'm afraid."

"But, why *not*? The felines stood no nonsense. The crowds did not gather. They'd be chased away. There's too much traffic now and it's interfering with our quality of life. It's maddening."

The haplessly tame animals constantly solicited my advice. They asked question after question. "How do we interact with the new human migrants if and when they arrive? How do we interact with the animals of the sea? How do we master the great seas? What do we do about the restlessness of the young ones who want to explore and migrate to the New Lands?"

Their incessant whining riled me. Did they not realise that I was as clueless as they were? My fuse became progressively shorter. Eventually,

I threw my restraint overboard. I gave them a piece of my mind when I started to express my contempt for their small-mindedness.

One day, George the Fox and the Council consulted me.

"Chief Miaow, we have a problem. Nobody's in command here. There's chaos wherever you look. We need strong leadership. Someone who can impose discipline and give a meaning to all this mayhem. We need a king and we want you to be that king. Your word will be law."

"I can never be king. If anything, we should offer the crown to General Jack. He is worthy of kingship, not I."

"Granted. But the General has left…"

"He will return. He said so. He keeps his promises. He will lead us to safety again. He will create order out of the chaos in a way only he can."

"What if he doesn't ever return?"

"He will return. I know it."

"What if he's dead?"

"Don't be silly. Men like him *never* die. They live on forever." I bristled.

"But that *is* the past, Miaow. You're stuck in the past. We have to look to the future."

"I see the past in the future. That way the future makes sense."

With each passing day, I became more unreasonable and irritable. The other animals expected much of me but I disappointed them. I was not capable of organising the circle of life in any effective constructive way. I sulked because of my glaring limitations. I was no longer able to influence the course of events as in General Jack's time. Frustration set in. I avoided society. I lost my appetite not only for food but also for life in general. I was unfulfilled, useless. I came across as apathetic and withdrawn.

How ironic! I always dreamt of being King of Our Land. I fantasized about how I would administer justice. Now that my dream came true, I had no interest in living the dream. General Jack had warned me that it was an impossible dream. How far seeing he was!

Relations were not much better with my family members.

Sabine was the first to notice I was out of sorts. She earnestly tried to console me, but it only made matters worse. To her credit, she backed off. She must have had an inkling about the genesis of my behaviour; because she then faded into the background and supported me by proxy. She pushed Jackat into my path. It was subtle of her. Sometimes, I wondered whether the ancestry of foxes ran in her blood.

The family rued my transition into a grumpy recluse. I constantly snapped at my family members whenever they tried to comfort me. My abrasive reactions to the well-intentioned overtures of my loved ones mortified me. I did my best to make up but I could not help it. I continued to snap at them. Had I become impossible to live with? My family members worried about me.

Twinkle my daughter repeatedly egged me on.

"Dad, why are you behaving so?"

"I can't suffer gladly those fools anymore."

"But Dad, you are the moral authority in Our Land. Animals are shying away from approaching you with their problems. They know you'd bite their heads off."

She continued,

"The other day, a dog without a nose asked me to intercede for him with you. He was exploring the beach. Down at the waterline, he saw a small crawling rock with *a hundred* legs emerging from either side. The dog was curious, so he hopped off to sniff at it. This rock stopped and with two large pincer claws snapped off the dog's nose. The dogs now demand guidance from you on how to interact with the creatures of the sea. They are perplexed. I don't blame them. They don't want to end up with bloodied noses."

"How should I know? Anyway, it serves that dog right. You should have told him not to be presumptuous. He shouldn't be poking his nose into unknown matters that do not concern him."

"*Dad...* What's come over you? Talking about interaction, Porky the chief of the pigs asked me for your advice. A posse of pigs saw a human walking. They rushed to him. They wanted to befriend him. This human, picked up rocks and threw them at the pigs to chase them away. They are at a loss on how to engage with the humans. You are the best person to address their concerns given you were so intimate with one yourself."

"With that filthy stench, I'm not surprised. Those pigs should have washed themselves before making the advance."

"Dad, you're not being helpful. Will you meet Porky?"

"Oh dear! *No!* From his stench, may the heavens deliver me, *please!*" I implored, rolling my eyes skyward. "How can I? Porky *stinks* to the high heavens. He's the stench of stenches. I keep smelling the stench for days after our meetings. The memory of his disgusting odour is enough to put me off food for weeks."

Twinkle sighed and shook her head in disapproval. She stared at me coldly. I knew she was obsessed with cleanliness. After the felines departed, she washed at least twelve times a day. She did not look kindly on Porky's legendary lack of hygiene. That is the reason why he was appointed chief of the pigs. The fierce felines never touched Porky, his stench repelled them. Under Feline Rule, the other pigs used to cluster around him to benefit from the protective range of his unpleasant smell.

But then, Twinkle said, "Dad, you're not being helpful, are you?" Her ire was directed at me, not at Porky.

"Twinkle, I have no answers, only questions like them. General Jack was the only one who had the answers. If he were here, he'd know what to do."

"But, he's not here, Dad. The onus is now on you. Why are you escaping from the responsibility?"

"I can't do it, Twinkle. It's just not in me. These exertions have drained me. I'm an empty shell. The General used to act through me."

"It was still *you* who acted then. Surely, that part of you can act, now. It's not that you can't do it; you *don't* want to do it. That's the way we see it."

"You don't understand."

"Do you know what everyone is saying about you? It upsets me and Purr so much. It's unjust, but on the other hand, your behaviour is fuelling their vile gossip. Oh, Dad do something! We were so proud of you. We used to look up to you so much. We love you. What can I do for you? How can I help?"

"Nothing. I don't want to talk about it. It's best we don't talk about it anymore." I slinked out of the hut while her back was turned.

"Dad, Dad?...*Dad!*" reached my ears as I was a few paces away. I suppressed a cynical chuckle. Twinkle must have twirled round to find the room empty.

A day later my son, Captain Purr called on me. He was thoughtful and upset about something. I invited him in. He was diffident, so I encouraged my hesitant son to say his piece.

"What's ailing you, son? Can I help in anyway?"

Purr did not reply He shuffled on the spot with downcast eyes.

"Well, son?"

He finally opened up. It was not about him or Sabine, though. It was all about me. I was his problem.

Purr pleaded with me, "Dad, what's wrong with you? Why are you avoiding us? Is there anything we can do for you? Both Twinkle and I are so worried."

"This does not concern you, son. Stay out of it."

"How can I?"

"Look, General Jack entrusted me with a responsibility. It was easy when he was around. I received the credit that was due to him. I merely did everything he said, down to the slightest detail. Now that he's gone, I don't know what to do. I've failed. I'm not cut out for this. I avoid everyone because I don't want to reveal my incompetence. I do it for your sakes' and for the family's honour. I don't want to be remembered as a fraud."

"You succeeded then. You achieved the impossible. It should be easier now. If you put your mind to it, you'll succeed again. You just have to pull yourself together. I know you can do it."

"You don't understand, son."

"What is there to understand, Dad. It's as clear as daylight. This is not the real you."

"What do you know about that?"

"Look Dad. If it's about Scratchy, we know how badly you took his death. Twinkle and I, we grieve as much as you do. We miss him. He was such a charismatic character, but life has to go-"

"Look, just shut up. You know nothing," I hissed and darted out of the room.

The sheep had long tried to attract my attention. I snubbed them. One day, Purr showed up in my hut.

"Dad, the sheep have asked me to pass on a message. The foxes are harassing them. A day does not go by when at least, one sheep does not go missing. They want to organise a vigilante force. They need your help. There's no security for them. We need a policing force to catch the rustlers. Law and order needs to be re-established."

The commonplace view of the forest outside the window was not impressive. The throbbing headache I had all morning intensified.

"Dad, you're not listening."

"Hmm?"

"I said the sheep need your expertise. Will you help out?"

"I don't see how I can make a difference."

"Oh! Come on. Nobody in Our Land is more qualified. You were the co-founder and leader of the Union Jacks. *Everyone* knows it."

The ensuing silence was interrupted by Purr's frustrated voice, "Will you or won't you help them?"

"I wonder what Twinkle is preparing for dinner-"

"Dad, don't change the subject. Will you help them or not?"

"No, I won't."

"But why?"

"Because I won't."

"Why not?"

I erupted, "Because they are fools. That's why," and I stormed out.

There was a morning when I loitered outside Purr's hut. Twinkle and Purr were inside conversing in agitated tones unaware that I was within earshot.

Twinkle lamented sobbing, "I'm *so* worried about Dad. He shuns me; he shuns everyone. The more I try to engage with him, the angrier he becomes. He's so irritable. He's not eating. Yesterday I prepared his favourite dish. He used to gobble it up. Now he doesn't touch it. He goes missing for days on end. He says he goes on search expeditions for the General, because Dad wants to rescue him from the darkness of the Dark Land. After all these years, imagine! He wants to enlighten the General with the good news. He gets incensed because no one will join him on his futile search parties. He can't understand how they can be so indifferent, ungrateful and so selfishly petty after all the General did for them. Before, he used to grumble because no one joined him on the search expeditions he organised in the eastern fringes of Our Land. Now, he's even venturing alone into the western borderlands of the Dark Land. Would you believe it? He's convinced that the General has fallen into a trap and he wants to rescue him. At this rate, it's Dad who will fall into a deadly trap. We'll lose him forever, Purr. Dad's neglecting himself. He's losing weight; his peel has lost its silky sheen. He's not washing enough.

"He's behaving irrationally. I'm at my wits' end. I myself, will go mad as well, worrying about him. I don't know what more to do for him."

Then she broke down and wailed, "Please *do* something, Purr."

Purr said, "He's a shadow of his former glorious self. I can't make him out anymore. Him and me, we can't get through to each other now. He rebuffs my attempts to reason with him. He's happy only when alone, brooding. I'll ask Jackat to shadow him. Dad enjoys his company. Dad fascinates Jackat. On the other hand, Jackat is restless. It might do them both a world of good."

Twinkle and Purr, bless them, could not be more different from me. Twinkle was a frivolous, well-meaning extrovert. Purr was unimaginative, staid but reliable. However, neither of them was in the same league of my dead son. General Jack had called Scratchy "the Son of Thunder", and so said all of us. Scratchy had been the creative force behind the Month of the Seven Missions. He had earned the moniker of "Blue Thunder" among his Union Jack comrades because when he struck, he was as unpredictable as a thunderbolt out of the serene blue sky. My three children were the sweet, the slow and the fast. I cherished all three. But Sabine was a combination of them all. Truly, she was a blessing in more ways than one and I owed it all to my dear wife's intercession. Sabine was a marvellous gift from the heavens. I had much to be grateful for. Yet I was unhappy and restless. Why was that?

Ironically, Purr's proposal concerning Jackat was a masterstroke. Jackat then, was a blossoming kitten whose emerging traits resembled Scratchy's more than anyone else. The more time I spent with him, the more I admired him. It was as if I was conversing with a reincarnated

Scratchy. My fondness of him grew each day. He was to be a tremendous comfort in my later years.

The truth was that the inner white cat was dying. Previously, General Jack's presence nurtured it. This demanding entity needed constant sustenance. Now it was withering. It was parched and desiccated. It was wasting away. The innate grey cat was taking over again. That pained me. I constantly thought of ways to revive the white cat in vain.

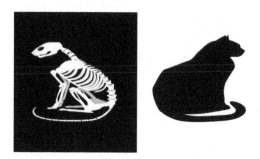

The older generation continued to respect and honour me until my dying day. The survivors of the Battle of the Five Kingdoms though, were shrinking in number. It was different with the emerging younger generation. These had become indifferent to me. I had become irrelevant in the daily management of the circle of life in Our Land. The inconvenient truth was that I, like everyone else, was a follower. None of us had leadership qualities. Not even George the fox. He had the guile but he did not have the brute force to rein in all the other animals. He could never command the respect needed for kingship.

II

A group of young cows approached me once.

"Chief Miaow, there was a group of erect two-legged human animals the other day. We introduced ourselves but they ignored us. What can we do to get their attention?"

"How should I know?"

"But our elders tell us you know everything. You were full of ideas."

"Those ideas were not mine. They were General Jack's."

"Who is General Jack?"

"General Jack was a great man. He led the revolt against Feline Rule," I bellowed.

"Oh! Our elders tell us he never existed. He was merely a symbol which the real heroes of the resistance brandished, to rally the animals. They also say that you were the key rallying figure. Only you can sort out this mess, now that the heroes have departed for the new green lands."

I glared at them. "What else do the elders tell you?" I asked in an irritated tone.

"Oh! The heroes were those valiant chargers of the Western, Eastern and Southern Trains. They fearlessly confronted the formidable enemy. They chased the enemy out of the land to the ends of the world."

A few weeks later, a group of fox elders visited me. George the fox was not among them.

"Chief Miaow, we have recommended that you are titled for your role in the Battle of the Five Kingdoms together with the other heroes."

"What heroes?"

"Well, the heroes of the Western, Eastern and Southern Trains, of course."

"As far as I can recall, there was *only* one hero."

"You refer to George the fox?"

"*Of course not!*" there was loathing in my voice, "I refer to General Jack."

They retorted, "The debacle of the battle was the fault of General Jack. He drew up battle plans that could never work. At the assembly, everyone had contested his various military strategies. The General had suppressed all opposition. He rubbished the most plausible battle plan proposed by George the fox. In fact, George's *blitzkrieg* battle plan won liberation for us."

"How can you say that? It's *not* true." I was indignant.

"The General was a dangerous, irresponsible boy. He almost provoked a violent feline crackdown upon us. Thankfully, George the fox forced the General's hand. He saved the entire resistance campaign that the General was on the verge of scuppering. Some considered the General a double agent in the pay of the lions. And with good reason. He was responsible for countless deaths of our fellow animals. When the going got tough, he fled like a coward."

"How dare you say these words? Please leave. I have nothing more to say to you foxes." I shoved them out one by one. I slammed the door in their faces. Livid with rage, I remained standing with my back pressed against the door, steamed up and hyperventilating. I stared defiantly at the wall. I was at war with the world. It took me a couple of hours to regain my composure. After I let off the steam, I remained distracted, bad tempered and hostile for the rest of the day. I was twitchy all week.

In recompense, they proposed to name me Chief Miaow the Great. What's so great about me? Nothing! We are nothing! What on earth were they thinking of? It goes without saying, I publically refused the accolade. Any claim I had to greatness rested in my ability to recognise the potential in General Jack's personality. He deserved the title not me. The great figures are those whose acts echo through the ages. He achieved the victory for us. He rocked the world. I merely helped him to midwife a new world but he created the new world.

The animals were sweeping the memory of General Jack aside. It became fashionable to belittle the role General Jack played in our liberation. Some even had the cheek to say he was not a hero. General Jack had made the extraordinary seem deceptively ordinary. That was his indisputable gift. The result of his feat was phenomenal. It was unparalleled. He split animal time in two.

The propagandists revisited the subject of the Battle of the Five Kingdoms. In the initial years, this subject was taboo. No one wanted to reveal his or her embarrassing presence in that farcical battle that never was. The version of the historic event was then manipulated. Now, everyone was a "hero". The propagandists even altered the order of the compartments in the Western, Eastern and Southern Trains. In their version, the fleeing cowering feline enemy occupied the front compartment whereas the following compartments were bristling with the fearsome allied heroes who chased them out of Our Land into permanent exile. They maintained the General was dangerous to our cause. The animals alone had overturned Feline Rule and banished the felines forever. They did it despite him, not because of him.

The Truth was under attack. The Great Lie had supplanted the Truth. Self-important animals who had most to gain - animals like George the fox and his associates - propagated this historical revision. However, there were many others too. They wanted to improve or advance their position in the new circle of life. These animals were ambitious but they had a conflict of interest. They themselves knew that none of them could ever become king. Not one of them had it in him to be king. But they were enthusiastic kingmakers. The kingmaker derives the same benefits of power that a king holds, maybe more. These propagandists were desperate to canvass for any candidate who had the personal traits suitable for kingship. No such candidate existed since the Battle of the Five Kingdoms. Thus, the king's throne remained vacant.

I could not stand by, doing nothing. There was a concerted all-out attack on the Truth. A new kind of battle raged, a bloodless one. I had to be the Defender of the Truth. I had a duty to preserve it as a treasury for the sake of those animals interested in the unadulterated Truth. How can the new generation tackle the future if they could not understand the past? They would merely repeat the mistakes of the past. This was a battle for the hearts and minds of the animals. Whoever won it controlled the lives of all the animals in the realm. As General Jack had predicted, the victors would acquire absolute power to rule the animal world.

I had to challenge and expose this propaganda as lies. If I did not do it, no one else would. I resolved to keep General Jack's legacy alive by writing the memoirs you are reading in the form of a journal. It was a thankless and hopeless task. I was to pursue that task until my dying day. Mine was a lone voice taking it out against an infinite contrary voice. This was to be my new mission. The injustice of the great Lie galvanized me out of my self-defeatist state of mind. I found satisfaction in battling for the truth, although I became a figure of ridicule and derision.

This was the only way I could help the new circle of life. I had to expound on the wisdom of General Jack. The journal will be a useful tool for the younger generation to avail of, when addressing the challenges of the new world. My ineffectiveness had previously relegated me to the outermost circumference of the circle of life. As a Defender of the Truth, I was reborn. I became a mover and shaker within the animal world. I was back in the centre of the circle of life. Not as a doer like in the past but as a moral authority.

III

I wrote the journal over the next ten years. General Jack had not yet found the safe place for us. I was the only one who constantly looked out for him. I spent the waking hours at the W-shaped tree reflecting, writing and waiting. The other animals passed by. They stopped in their tracks to stare at me with smirking faces. After a few minutes, they nonchalantly strode off shaking their heads. There were too many deniers of the Truth around. They mocked me. Old age made me set in my ways. Old habits die hard. I was always thin-skinned by nature and detractors affronted me. Bitterness set in. I retaliated with abusive invective against my detractors. I did not seem to be making much headway in my new mission. There were not many seekers of the Truth around. I floated in a sea of indifference.

General Jack had become my holy grail. I knew it was there but I could not find it. The younger generation believed that General Jack never existed. They considered him a myth or a figment of our imagination. The young ones, who never met him, believe only what they see, feel and touch. They referred to me as the sole leader of the resistance who sadly, had become touched in the head after the initial catastrophe of the Battle of the Five Kingdoms.

General Jack once mused, "What will happen if the Overlords were to be eliminated?"

I replied, "Well, obviously we will rule ourselves."

Then he said, "There will remain a vacuum which will be filled by other masters. You just replace one with the other. One will be as despotic as the other."

I thought it was good that the upper powerful classes of the other Four Kingdoms had settled in the New Lands. They would have lorded it over us just like the lions. The problem is none of us domesticated animals are powerful enough to rule the land. We match each other in strength. We are too submissive. Some are more stupid than others. Some are bright. There are the indifferent animals and there are the selfish ones. Can the new humans become our new Overlords? If they resemble General Jack, they will be good and fair leaders.

How we missed the guidance of General Jack! Ridding ourselves of the Feline Overlords in retrospect looked easy. Rebuilding and adapting to the new reality was much more difficult. One thing is certain though. I will ensure the legacy of General Jack lives on forever. In the children's stories, we will name many heroes and protagonists after him. In the adult world, many great military commanders will emulate his military strategies.

IV

The journal is practically finished. I want to write the last lines at the W-shaped tree. It is dusk. The sky is indigo-tinged, just like when I had my first apparition of General Jack. I am old and rickety now. I am very tired but I must make the effort. I have to be there when General Jack arrives to tell him that he won after all. Better late than never. It's the least I could do for him after all he did for us. I sit down. The journal is finished. It's so thick, it looks more like a book. I remember that I have not yet decided whether to title the book "The Four Ways of Life" or … I turn my head sideways to nostalgically scrutinize the eastern horizon one last time. My dim eyes well up. Behind me, there is the sudden loud rustling of leaves. I have to see who there is, but I do not have the strength to turn my head. I am so weary. I'm an empty shell, drained. I hear my constant refrain, *"Surely, he'll come. Surely, he'll*

come. Surely, he'll come…" monotonously whispered under my laboured breath. My mind is blank. The horizon is blurred. I try to write but my eyes become too heavy, as does my hand…

CHAPTER 13

THE FIRST SUNRISE

$\mathfrak{I}$ Am Captain Purr. I am the elder son of Chief Miaow. I was one of the Union Jacks in the days of the resistance. That morning, I did my usual check on Dad. His hut was empty. He did not sleep in it last night. *Oh no! Dad. Don't die on us, please don't!* I imagined the worst.

I ran over to Twinkle's place in a panic. *I must not reveal my agitation. I mustn't raise false alarms. She'll take it badly.* I paused outside her door for a few moments to catch my breath and to regain my composure. She was washing herself. "Twinkle, have you seen Dad?" I calmly asked.

"No. Is something wrong?"

"Oh! Nothing special." I said casually, "I have a message for him from the Council, that's all. They need some advice."

Twinkle let out a groan.

"Try down by the brook. Jackat's playing there. Dad might be with him."

I dashed off, but he was not with Jackat.

"Grandad is probably at the W-shaped tree waiting for the General's return, as always. He must have gone earlier than usual. I'll be joining him later." Jackat said.

"Yesterday, Miaow said he wanted to look his best, because the General was coming."

"He says that every day, Dad."

I mustn't reveal my concern to Jackat. It would destroy him. They're so close. I slowly walked away with a leisurely air.

Once I was out of Jackat's sight, I sprinted to the W- shaped tree where deep down, I always knew father would be. Please Dad, don't leave us now. What will we do without you? You've given us so much. Please don't die. Stay with us a little longer. Agonizing thoughts rushed through my mind between each gasp.

I arrived at the far end of the enclosure and I stopped. *Oh, thank goodness! There he is. Alive and well.* I regained my breath and with a relieved smile approached him at a relaxed pace from the rear. The tree trunk partly interfered with my vision.

He was sleeping. There was a content smile on his face. "Dad?" I coolly called. "Dad!" I repeated in a stronger voice… "Dad! *Dad!*" I stressed in an agitated tone… He did not reply. Nor did he move. "*Dad, Dad,*" I shrieked as I nudged him. *Oh no! He's dead, no, no…no!* I crumbled beside him sobbing. Time stood still as one soul gazed at the other with overflowing affection. A stream of emotional thoughts flowed inside but I struggled to process any of them.

Father always had an obsession about survival because the worth of an animal under Feline Rule was judged by his or her life expectancy. Our safety - mine, Twinkle's, Sabine's - had always been uppermost in his fretful mind. We had all outlived our peers, by no means an easy feat, and we owed it all to father's daily painstaking efforts to keep us out of danger. He did this despite his shy nature.

He had passed away peacefully in his sleep. In his right hand, he held the feather pen. It was one of the feathers of the ill-fated standard of the Army of the South. Ironically, father considered it our good luck charm. He believed it was the magic wand of Lady Luck. He boasted that she had graciously rode on that gust of wind to visit us. He used to say that General Jack always wondered whether she would pay us a visit during the battle.

In the other hand, he clasped to his bosom what he called his book of wisdom. I gently released these two items from his hands to write these last lines.

I must return home to tell the others. I've got to break it gently to them. I retraced my steps to call father's family but I stopped. The prompt recollection of a baffling observation ruffled me - the expression on Dad's face. I looked back at father's face. Funny! That expression was familiar but I could not place it.

We returned together with my son Jackat, whom we had named after our General. We agreed to hold a dignified private burial by his revered W-shaped tree. We buried him next to Scratchy. We did not announce his death publicly. The news of his death would have reverberated to the ends of Our Land. We did not want huge crowds irreverently trampling over this hallowed ground where our liberation movement was born. We were convinced Dad would have concurred with our funeral arrangements.

As soon as we arrived, Twinkle stared at Dad through her tear stained eyes. She promptly remarked, "Father has not had that content look on his face since General Jack departed. Not even in the victory celebrations did he have that look!"

In an instant, it all fell into place. General Jack had returned after all! He had kept his promise! Dad was there to greet him as he had always wished. All this time, General Jack had been waiting for his faithful comrade-in-arms in the Great Beyond. They were together again! Dad was in a better place. With moist eyes, I looked up at the sun rising over the mountains. The new day had just begun for Miaow.

II

Sabine was seriously ill. She had given birth to two newborns. We named them Scratcher and Miaow Miaow. But Sabine remained ill. She was in severe pain and febrile. A few days later, we realised how serious her condition was when she delivered three stillborns. These had long been dead and previously trapped inside her womb. She had lost plenty of blood. Severe post-delivery infection and inflammation ailed her. Sabine's physical condition was poor, she could not raise her head off the bed. Twinkle nursed her and constantly washed her. She insisted that the washing would scare away the tiny invisible demons that were trying to drag Sabine away from us into the underworld. It did not help. Sabine's dire condition continued to deteriorate.

Sabine had one last wish, she wanted to visit her Papi's grave. She pleaded with me. I feared the long painful journey might kill her. I told her she needed absolute rest. She told me to promise that if she died, she would be buried between her Papi and myself. She said we were the two dearest people in her life. I could not but give in to all her demands.

The following morning was a windy day. We set out despite Twinkle's vehement protestations. I wrapped her up in a warm leaf shawl and I gently carried her in my arms. I walked the long walk slowly as I did not want to cause her pain because of the jolting movements. She did not take her tearful, affectionate eyes off me.

After a few steps when we were alone in the wild, unexpectedly, Sabine raised her head off my chest. Her eyes shifted here and there. Her ears kept turning in various directions. Her whiskers twitched repeatedly. "Purr dear, can you hear the voices?" she inquired.

"What voices?" I asked mechanically.

"There are voices in the wind. The words are floating on the wind. They're being carried away by the wind. You're sure you can't hear them, dear? I hear two types of voices and they are very familiar to both of us."

"Really! What sort of voices are they?"

"Sshh!"

Throughout the long journey, Sabine was in a trance. Her ears kept moving, picking the sound waves. She was so distracted; she was in another world. But she was very much alive and alert, more focused than before. Her body was no longer floppy. It tensed up and she absently squeezed my arms. When we arrived at the W- shaped tree, I laid her down by her Papi's grave. She lay there motionless, silent, tears streaming down her face. Her ears kept twitching. This went on for a couple of hours.

I stepped back and stood guard silently over her in case she needed anything. She was in ecstasy and I wanted to ensure that nothing or anyone would interrupt her state of mind. The colour returned to her face. She looked the best she had been for some time. She sat erect glowingly radiant, almost transfigured. She repeatedly jerked her upturned head as though she was trying to capture unseen particles in the air with her ears.

Suddenly the wind died down. After a few minutes of swaying her head to and fro in different positions, she cried, "I can't hear them anymore," and she collapsed.

I rushed to her. She was exhausted and she wept. "I can't hear them anymore. They were Papi and the General. They were talking about us. I can't hear them anymore..." Sabine was hot and drenched. I carried her home. She had always been imaginative. Besides, now she was delirious.

She rested in bed and slept for two days. Twinkle and I took turns watching over her. I did not want Jackat to see her in this state. At his tender age, it would have been too traumatic for him. Her slow death might have conditioned him for the rest of his life.

On the third day, Sabine rose from her bed. She was weak but she looked brighter. She wanted to talk to me. She grabbed both of my paws in hers and said, "Purr dear, I want to tell you something important. Please don't laugh at me and don't interrupt me."

"My lips are sealed, Sabine."

She nodded and smiled wanly. She caressed my cheek tenderly with her paw.

"I'm convinced I overheard a conversation between Papi and the General. I am sure of the voices. The original conversation was like an intact jigsaw puzzle. The strong winds must have broken up the puzzle and scattered the various pieces or words across my path. So, I heard the many different individual words in their real voices. I did not hear the actual entire conversation. Each and every word or sound that repeatedly fluttered around me, is imprinted in my mind. I now have to put the words together as best as I can, to reconstruct the whole conversation. It will take time and patience. Will you stand by me, dear? Anyone else will think I'm crazy but I know I'm right. I just need time to break the code. I know I can do it."

Sabine worked on it for seventy-two days, trying myriad different combinations in her fervent mind. During this time, she practically lived in a parallel world. She was in a state of rapture, her eyes always moist and bloodshot. Her physical condition perceptibly improved. Her appetite increased. The pain decreased. The fever subsided. She started walking. She wished to spend the day by the W-shaped tree because that's where she felt closest to her Papi. She said she could work better there. Initially, I used to accompany her and loiter while she worked.

Later, she was well enough to go by herself. But I always followed at a safe distance unseen, just in case something happened to her. Since the breakup of the Five Kingdoms, Our Land had become a much safer place. But although she looked well, I was not entirely sure she was all there, both physically and mentally. During these waiting periods, I wondered.

On the seventy-second day she called me. "Purr, dear," she said with tears in her eyes. "I've cracked the code."

"Sabine, I keep wondering. How do you know that it is the true conversation or that the conversation really exists? How do you know it's not a figment of your imagination? Are you really as well as you look? Are you in the right frame of mind? I'm *very* worried about you. I don't know what to expect."

She nodded, "I feel it inside - the warm, glowing feeling which knows the conversation's genuine. You will know as well, on hearing it, whether the conversation is true or not."

"Purr, this was how the conversation went…

"I heard running footsteps. Papi was exclaiming repeatedly in an excited voice, 'You won! You won! You won!… I've *been* wanting to tell you that you won!' Then, he sobbed uncontrollably. There were no more footsteps but I heard a soft thumping sound as though Papi was banging on the General's chest. It could be that Papi was pressed against the General's bosom.

"Then, I heard The General's voice saying softly, 'sshh!... sshh!..sshh! !... I know, I know, I *always* knew.' There was a swishing sound as though the General was comforting Papi by caressing his back with his hand.

"Next, the General said in a gentle but firm voice, 'No, Miaow! *You* won!'

"Then, I heard Papi wailing again like a child, exclaiming from the depth of his heart in a cracking voice, 'We won! We won! We won!' The swishing sound of caressing continued. Throughout, the General must have held Papi in a locked embrace, constantly rocking him gently. I say this because Papi's words were muffled and the loudness of the words varied. His face must have been resting on the General's bosom.

"This is how I reconstructed the scene in my mind. On unexpectedly getting a glimpse of the General, Papi must have run into the General's arms to break the good news. He was overjoyed but he could not contain his joy. The emotions of the long delayed reunion must have been too much for Papi. He broke down in tears and he pounded his pent-up joy on the General's bosom. The General would have embraced him and Papi must have clung to him. They may have conversed intermittently in that locked pose for some time or at least, until Papi's release reaction was expended. During this time, the General was trying to comfort Papi and

to soothe his fears. I think Papi regained his composure; but he had difficulty maintaining it or stopping his tears, because he kept sniffing and at times his voice broke.

"Finally, the background sounds stopped. I think they were sitting side by side on the grass. The General said, 'I am taking you home, Miaow.'

"Papi asked, 'But *where* is home?'

"The General replied, '*I am* home.'

"Papi asked plaintively, 'But, will I be left *alone* again?' His voice was strained.

"The General replied, '*Never!* Never again! My home is your home. Not many have made the journey, but you have. *You* won your race.'

"Then, Papi asked, 'What will become of Jackat?'

"The General replied, 'He can take care of himself. He knows what to do. You prepared him well. He will not let you down. He will do you proud. But that is another story.'

"Then, Papi said, 'How could a plodder like me produce such a masterpiece of life, as Jackat? Through Sabine, he has Scratchy's gifts and, in addition, he has Purr's solid staying power. I always wished to be like that.'

"The General replied, 'You have to be careful what you wish for, as you may acquire it in the end. With soulful faith like yours, Miaow, you'd move the mountains in your world. Such is the force of the prayer that you practised each day of your life. Your heartfelt perseverance is simply irresistible.'

"There was a pause and then I heard footsteps. Both the voices and the footsteps became fainter. They must have been walking together in a direction away from me. I could not make out most of the words as they became fainter and fainter. Papi was in a vivacious, bouncy mood. He seemed to be bombarding the General with petitions and supplications. It was only Papi's voice I heard though, chatting away excitedly.

The only words I could make out were: 'I wish…. Purr'; 'I wish…. Sabine'; 'I wish …. Twinkle'; 'Where ……Scratchy…..'; 'Wife….forgive….'

"And then I heard no more voices."
And I wondered no more.

In weakness, my strength,
In defeat, my victory,
In darkness, the light,
In death, new life.

Chief Miaow

CHAPTER 14

MIAOW'S JOURNEY

I

My name is Jackat. Chief Miaow was my grandfather. Five years have passed since his death. I have to keep Miaow's flame alive for future generations. General Jack, whom I never met, lit the flame. I was born one year after the Battle of the Five Kingdoms. Grandad had become a difficult person, but I was one of the few whose company he enjoyed. He was fond of me. Maybe it was because Mum and Dad named me after General Jack. He shared his loneliness with me because I was the only person who understood his inner journey. No one else understood him, not even my father. No one could come to grips with his irrational behaviour.

Every day, Mum and Aunt Twinkle despatched me with food for Grandad. I regularly checked on Grandad when he scribbled under the W-shaped tree. We conversed there for hours. I read his journal as he wrote it. The animated discourses I had with Grandad were no different to the ones General Jack held with the younger star-struck Miaow. Only, now I was the wide-eyed pupil, he was the mentor. Likewise, these discussions had a profound impression on me. They moulded my character and my outlook to life. With time, I formed my impressions on the nature of the protagonists' personalities during the liberation.

II

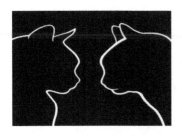

Miaow was a weak character replete with flaws. In the pre-war period, he displayed a lack of initiative despite being opinionated. He was prejudiced and had no sympathy for certain undesirables, like the snakes and Noisy the crazy parrot. He was also unforgiving. Grandad was quick to point an accusing finger when things went awry, for instance, against the elephants or gazelles. He could be spiteful and almost executed the scouting birds and the parrot when they crossed him.

Why did General Jack single Miaow out for being special? Miaow was the only one in Our Land who had an inner voice. It was not a passing whimsical voice, it was a well formed conscience. Everyone else in Our Land was, well, just an animal. Miaow did not acknowledge it, though he moaned about the nameless feeling that never gave him rest. My maternal grandmother (who I never knew) noted it as she lay dying. She had spoken her prophetic words just before she expired. Miaow never understood the significance of her statements.

War brings out the best or the worst in a character. In Miaow's case, it begot his nobility of spirit. Injustice roused him into an enterprising cat prepared to fight for his principles. Under the inspirational guidance of General Jack, he delivered on all fronts. More importantly, the newfound sense of mission ignited the three cardinal virtues of life in him – faith, hope and charity. With regards to the latter value, he scored high in friendship but otherwise, persistently fell short. His relations with, for instance, his family, his critics or supplicants were far from charitable. He vented his frustrations on them. Even during the war years he remained conflicted. He shared General Jack's empathy for Champ, despite his treachery. For Miaow, Champ the monkey was a tragic figure, a good soul who had lost his way. Miaow's heart went out to him. By contrast, he could not understand why the treachery of Olaf the wolf and George the fox was not punished. He poured scorn on the crazy parrot and was resentful over the choice of such a hapless creature as an assassin. Although he was aware of Noisy's harmlessness, he almost executed him.

In the post-war years, Miaow's character degenerated again, sinking to a level lower than in the pre-war years. He lost his motivation and became conscious of his ineptness. The weakness of character came to the fore again, as he slid down a spiral of low self-esteem and self-pity. This culminated in a protracted depression, of which he showed all the characteristic symptoms. If he had had access to drugs or alcohol, he might have drowned his sorrows in them. During the war, he had felt fulfilled and expectations were raised. After the war, he became aware that he could not fulfil those expectations. He considered himself a failure. Life lost its meaning for him, he was rudderless. He could not make sense of the pervading chaos and pettiness after the collapse of Feline Rule.

It was his strong sense of justice that redeemed him from this self-destructive spiral. In the mists of time, the Truth had become history. History became legend. Legend became myth. The myth became a malicious lie. This malevolent engineering of the truth irked him. For Miaow, organised slander was an injustice. Injustice once again rekindled the fire of the three cardinal virtues in his breast. He considered it another type of war and this brought out the best in him again. He redeemed himself by finding his vocation as the Defender of the Truth. In other words, he became the pioneering founder of journalism in the animal world. He became the first journalist of the New World.

Unknown to himself, he was fighting another battle as well - a personal battle (against his inner demons) within the battle for the Truth. He died in that renewed state of self-fulfilment. My aunt Twinkle remarked on his condition when he lay on his deathbed. It was not happiness. It was not joy. It was something much deeper and satisfying. *It was peace of soul.*

Once, Miaow referred to his inner secret garden. He said it had always been barren and unproductive. The soil was caked and parched. In it, he complained nothing grew apart from weeds. These never stopped growing. They let nothing else grow. They choked out any new

life. He cut them but they grew again. General Jack helped him clear out the garden and turn over the soil. The General added sustenance to the soil and planted a seed. Together, Miaow and the General tenderly nurtured the seed. It grew into a wonderful, colourful garden. Under their constant attention, it did not only grow. It flourished. The fragrance that the secret garden emitted was magical. All the non-feline animals picked up the

scent and fell under its spell. With fortitude and perseverance, Miaow painstakingly cleared the weeds, so his secret garden could thrive. He was so proud of it. He constantly referred nostalgically to those glorious days. Following the departure of General Jack, Miaow tried to keep it up. Despite his best efforts, the weeds grew and the secret garden wilted. He kept at it though. He never gave up but the back-breaking strain wore him down. Despite the endless presence of weeds, he found the impetus to make the garden grow. Although it could not attain its former splendour, he was content, nonetheless. He had done it by himself. He had managed to pick up the pieces and give renewed meaning to his life.

General Jack had set the bar high. By assiduously clinging to his coat tails, Miaow easily reached the standard. Once the General was gone, Miaow realised he could not reach that standard. Even worse, he could not even hold up that bar. The painful disillusion ate him up. In later life, he inadvertently found a new way of holding up a different type of bar for all to see. In so doing, he unwittingly managed to reach that standard which previously eluded him; and he regained his self-respect.

In the autumn of his life, Grandad downheartedly reminisced about his hard won victories and his gut wrenching defeats. Adversity can draw out talents that others would never have used or never imagined they possessed. Endurance was the only talent that Miaow cynically boasted about. He acknowledged it as the reason for his election as chief of the cats. But even in his wildly changing fortunes from the fertile peaks of success to the barren valleys of failure, he never gave due weight to his indisputable virtue of perseverance.

Miaow won the mother of all battles late in his life. It was victory over himself. It was the fulfilment of his destiny. Previously, he was dependent on General Jack for everything. Now, he did it on his own steam. He had matured to that extent, in spite of himself, only in his later years. He may have lost his battle for the Truth, as he was isolated. However, the unjust challenge on the part of the gullible and fickle masses reawakened the three cardinal virtues in him. Such is the collective power of these virtues, when sincerely practised, they vanquished his inner demons. This inner benevolent dragon swept the demons away and won the field for him. During this time, he remained hot tempered and intolerant, almost bigoted. These blinkered traits were the battle scars of his psychic wars compounded by righteous indignation. His personal triumph in the eternal struggle despite his flaws, rendered his inner victory all the more impressive. Now he has his eternal reward for which he worked so hard.

Miaow is the true hero of the saga. He was an ordinary cat who performed extraordinary acts against impossible odds.

III

George the fox was wise by nature. Miaow could appreciate wisdom though he was not wise. He developed that wisdom only in his later years. George was the consummate unprincipled opportunist. He used anyone as a means to an end. He knew he could never be king but he craved to be the power behind the throne. He did not care who was in that throne as long as he was the one to place the contender on the throne.

George was far sighted. Like Miaow, he saw the potential in General Jack. For Miaow, the General was the end in itself. Miaow indulged in hero worship. George was cynical. For him, General Jack was a means to an end. He used others out of self-interest. Everyone was expendable. He used Olaf the wolf and tried to use Miaow as well after the battle. George used them as pawns in his power games. After he attained what he could from the General, George plotted to have him removed. At that juncture, George acknowledged that what he desired was poles apart from what the General was toiling for. George wanted absolute power. The General was aspiring for co-existence and sharing of power. This is not dissimilar to the way the Roman Empire split up into nations. In this narrative, we see a hint of that happening in the aftermath of the Month of the Seven Missions - the carving out of the western tiger domain, the southern lion domain, the eastern cougar/panther/jaguar domain and another territory in the middle reserved for all the others.

Inwardly, Miaow acknowledged his incompetence. Yet he was honest and he admitted it. George the fox knew he was inadequate for the task, as indeed were all the survivors of the Battle of the Five Kingdoms. However, George tried to cover for his deficiencies by distorting the truth. He was dishonest and that riled Miaow's modesty.

George was also unscrupulous. When he found out about Olaf the wolf's plans, though he did not agree, he sought personal advantage from the assassination. He rationalised it. This cynicism contrasts with the sincerity and integrity of his innocuous feline rival. Miaow had no qualms about revealing his foolishness, when he rectified his misreporting of Noisy the crazy parrot's actions. Moreover, Miaow was humble enough to seek out the parrot and ask for his

pardon. This episode in itself, testifies to the reliability of Miaow the journalist's reporting.

IV

Miaow maintained the Battle of the Five Kingdoms split animal time in two. In his modesty, he credited General Jack solely for this historically sensational achievement. He was truthful as, after all, it was General Jack's doing. Miaow by himself, could not do it. But it was equally true that General Jack could not have succeeded without Miaow's loyal and decisive contribution. Grandad played a larger part than he was prepared to admit in begetting this great epochal event. He made the right crucial, inspired decisions at the right time. Providence did the rest. Grandad's serial decision-making was grudgingly hard for him, because it was countered by his timid, indecisive nature. He had a morbid fear of decisions because he was scared of the consequences, whatever they may be. It was in his character to forever put off decisions. But ironically, Grandad was the perfect receptacle and conduit through which amazing grace did its work.

The battlefields of the Battle of the Five Kingdoms mirrored Miaow's innate battleground. Before his association with General Jack, Miaow's behaviour was no different from that of the protagonists of the battle. Like him, they instinctively ran away from conflict and from danger. Although General Jack infused him with the courage to right the wrongs of the animal world, Miaow constantly struggled to beef up the flesh to match the exacting demands of his spirit. Insecurity continued to plague him. He did not trust himself. Nonetheless, he finally faced conflict head on. His seemingly futile, laborious efforts ultimately bore the fruit of eternal victory. Thus ended Chief Miaow's *sturm und drang* odyssey.

The onus is now on me to continue Miaow's journey. I have to pick up where he left off. He achieved so much for the animal world, but there is still much to be done. I have to extend to the animal world of my time, the meaning and sense of direction which Miaow cultivated in his inner self. Only that way, can the animal world bring order to the chaos of these muddled times.

In an age long forgotten, Miaow was the hero in a land of no heroes and he did it his way. His name is not difficult to remember, hard to forget.

General Jack and Miaow live on.
A fire burns within me.
Through me,
General Jack and Chief Miaow live on!

Victory may sometimes be disguised as defeat.

Henry Wadsworth Longfellow

177

APPENDIX

AUTHOR'S EXPLANATORY NOTES

I. NATURE AND WILD LIFE

Some curiosities concerning nature in the novel.

Did you know that?

- ◆ **#1.**Europe and Asia form one huge land mass called Eurasia, which is divided by the Ural Mountains. Russia (and Turkey) straddle both continents. The events of the book play out in Europe, west of the Urals and the Mesopotamian desert. The Dark Land is Asia.**(Page 8)**
- ◆ Europe is named after Europa- the wide gazing, broad faced princess in Greek mythology. Europe is considered the old continent. The people in it have migrated westward, eastward and southward, in the directions of mother Europa's far seeing gaze, to colonize the outlying continents.
- ◆ It is possible that the wild life of the old continent migrated in a similar way in earlier times. The wild life of the old continent now consists mostly of domesticated or "tame" wild animals. The fiercer or more exotic animals reside outside Europe
- ◆ Panthers and Jaguars inhabit Latin America. Cougars and their black cousins-the pumas, share North American territory with the other descendants of the Western Train-the grizzly bears, the grey wolves, the coyotes, the moose and the bison. Elephants are distributed in the Far East together with the tigers. These are the heirs of the opposing armies of the Western battleground. Elephants also live in sub-Sahara Africa together with the other descendants of the Southern Train - the rhinos, hippos, hyenas, zebras, giraffes, gazelles and antelopes. This green land is also the habitat of the lions, cheetahs and leopards. The Sahara Desert is the home of camels. This fantasy adventure story explains how and why these exotic animals came to populate these lands.
- ◆ The python is found in Africa. It is not venomous but it kills its prey by constricting it. By contrast, the cobras and rattlesnakes (particularly the copperhead) are venomous. They are distributed in Asia and the Americas respectively. The viper is the only venomous snake in Europe.
- ◆ In ancient times known as the Ice Age, the oceans were frozen. It is posited that they melted because of global warming.

- The vibrations of underwater earthquakes generate a tsunami. In the past, they have also arisen as a result of meteorite impacts.
- Various theories have been proposed to account for the extinction of dinosaurs. The most plausible is a massive asteroid impact.
- The bulk of dinosaur remains have been exhumed in the Americas and in the Far East, predominantly North America and China respectively. Very few remains have been unearthed in Southern America or Europe, and then, these have been discovered almost exclusively in the south of England.
- Mammals, including elephants, suffer from red-green colour blindness.
- Lions fear elephants, rhinos, wolves and hippopotamuses. The lion dominates the cheetahs and leopards. Besides, tigers fear the lions and leave their food for them. The rhinos and the hippos are the most unpredictable and dangerous of animals. Their charges are particularly frightening.
- The elephant is uneasy in the presence of the mouse. The small agile mouse is able to evade the slow thumping steps of the elephant. The rodent climbs up the elephant's legs unseen, tickling and nibbling at its belly. The elephant is vulnerable and panics as it cannot swipe it off, nor can it ignore the mouse.

II. FAMOUS BATTLES

There is a saying *"History repeats itself."*

There is another saying, *"History does not repeat itself. It is the same history, never broken, never halted."*

Which saying is true?

There is a quote attributed to Mark Twain, *"History does not repeat itself, it rhymes."*

Can you see any parallels between the following military observations and the novel?

- ◆ **#1.**The cavalry decided the battles of the English Civil War. The royalist cavalry lead by the dashing Prince Rupert was superior, but too undisciplined. After a successful cavalry charge, they continued chasing the dispersed enemy for miles well out of the battlefield confines. When hours later they returned to the battlefield tired, the battle would be over. Their departure left a vacuum that was exploited by the slower but disciplined Cromwellian cavalry. These never left the confines of the battlefield and always regrouped to relaunch several new cavalry charges that ultimately overwhelmed the enemy. **(Page85)**
- ◆ **#2.**In the famous Battle of Austerlitz, Napoleon's *grande armée* fought the huge armies of three superpowers. He managed to keep the three armies separate, preventing them from linking up and defeated each army in turn.**(Page81)**
- ◆ **#3.**Napoleon used to reconnoitre the battleground himself incognito on the eve of the battle. He surveyed the terrain to position his army in a strategically favourable position with the intention of maximizing the devastating impact of his artillery. Moreover, Napoleon identified the disadvantageous area into which he manoeuvred the enemy army. The Duke of Wellington outdid him at Waterloo. Thunderstorms and heavy rainfall delayed the arrival of Napoleon's own troops. By the time his army arrived on the battlefield, Wellington's troops had already been deployed on a ridge in such a way that they

were protected from the full force of Napoleon's artillery.**(Page91)**

♦ **#4.**The main reason for Napoleon's defeat at Waterloo was the fact that one third of his army under General Grouchy went missing. This army never made it to the battlefield for reasons that are unknown to this day. Consequently, Napoleon's army was heavily outnumbered in the latter part of the battle.**(Page113)**

♦ **#5.**General Robert E. Lee fought ten major battles in the American Civil War. His armies were always heavily outnumbered and under-resourced. All these battles were defensive except Gettysburg. He never lost a defensive battle and inflicted massive losses on the Northern army. It is much easier for an underdog army to fight a defensive battle. At Gettysburg, the Confederates lost because there was lack of co-ordination between the main divisions, resulting in mistimed attacks.**(Page 95)**

♦ **#6.**At the Battle of Hattin in Palestine, the tumultuous famed charge of the Crusaders was nullified by the opening up of a wide passage in Saladin's Saracen forces, which allowed the entire cavalry to pass through into empty space. It was a futile all-or-nothing charge.**(Page 105)**

♦ **#7.**In the German wars of expansion, the wily Chancellor Bismarck deliberately provoked the naïve emperor Napoleon III into declaring war on Germany. He provided the French emperor with his *casus belli* or justification for war. This was the prelude for the disastrous Franco-Prussian War that was another humiliation for France. It heralded the decline of France as a military superpower. Karl Marx said about this nephew of Napoleon Bonaparte, *"Hegel reveals somewhere that all great world historical facts and personages appear, so to speak, twice. He forgets to add: the first time as tragedy, the second time as farce."***(Page 96)**

♦ **#8.**St Louis IX had the passionate desire to liberate the Holy Land from the occupation of the Saracen forces. He spent years preparing for this crusade ignoring the impatience of his peers. He was extremely methodical and orderly. He painstakingly laid down every minute detail of the campaign personally. When the army finally arrived in the Middle East, the entire campaign broke down practically overnight, mostly because of factors that were beyond the king's control. His army never made it into Palestine. He himself spent most of his time in Palestine as a prisoner rather than as a liberator.**(Page117)**

♦ **#9**.General George A. Custer was an accomplished young general who suffered a crushing defeat at the Battle of the Little Bighorn. This was the only major battle the American natives won in the Indian Wars. General Custard relied on outdated intelligence that drastically underestimated the size of the Indian army. That, together with the Yankees' overconfidence, ensured that the Indian braves coming at them from all angles, routed the Yankee army.**(Page93)**

♦ **#10**.In the Second World War, the British cracked the Enigma Code, through which the German high command communicated battle orders. From then onwards, the Allies won every battle including the decisive Battle of Britain that obliterated the *Luftwaffe*. The British Air Force knew every detail of the German aerial offensive in advance, including the time, coordinates and number of planes deployed. The *Luftwaffe*, on the other hand, were completely in the dark about the British operations. The only major victory of the *Wehrmacht* after the Enigma Code revelation was in the closing stages of the war – the counteroffensive Battle of the Bulge. This victory was attributed to the fact that the German commander involved did not make use of the Enigma Code in his communications. The allies were taken by surprise. **(Page43)**

♦ **#11**.Roman legions under the Emperor Septimius Severus were held back by scorpion bombs launched by the defenders of a Mesopotamian stronghold. Earthenware was loaded with scorpions. Under this incessant rain of scorpion bombs, the Roman legions finally broke off the attack and retreated. Likewise, during the Gaullist wars, the fierce Gauls launched beehives into the invading Roman armies.**(Page110)**

♦ **#12**.The Battle of Grunwald is the largest medieval battle that pitted the might of the Teutonic Knights against the Polish-Lithuanian Federation. The two armies faced each other on the battlefield, but neither army was prepared to launch the first attack. They remained inactive in the blistering heat for most of the day. The Poles were sheltered in the woods where they were protected from the famed awesome Teutonic heavy cavalry charges. The Teutonic Knights, on the other hand, had dug lines of defensive trenches before the main army. In order to induce the Polish troops out of the woods, the Grandmaster tried to provoke the Poles into launching the opening attack. He sent a taunting present of two swords to the Polish king with an insulting message. However, the Polish-Lithuanian Army did not budge. Finally, later in the day, the Poles fired the opening salvo with a feinted cavalry attack/retreat. The itchy Teutonic Knights fell for the ruse, unleashing a massive Teutonic onslaught that resulted in a decisive defeat for the Teutonic Knights. It precipitated the decline of the mighty Teutonic Knights as a military power and Poland regained its independence.**(Page110)**

What is the value of history?

Otto von Bismarck, *"What we learn from history is that no one learns from history."*

III. TYPES OF GOVERNMENT

What modes of government can you make out in the novel?
- ♦ Democracy is the rule by the majority. It respects the free will of the people. It has its flaws, as it does not necessarily mean that the majority is right. In addition, glitzy media manipulation can trick voters into voting for the wrong political party.
- ♦ Dictatorship is at the other end of the spectrum. It ensures unity and order but is flawed, as it does not respect free will. Power is concentrated in the hands of a small minority. Since it does not permit opposition, the rulers yield absolute power. Absolute power corrupts and is abusive.
- ♦ In Monarchy, a noble family based on blood ties (not based on merit) holds power indefinitely. The most powerful however, are the kingmakers, who are the powers behind the throne. It can be associated with feudalism where society is divided into strata, the lower strata being known as serfs. Most of the assets of the serfs belong to the state.
- ♦ Anarchy occurs when different irreconcilable factions develop in a country. These many factions resort to violence to resolve their differences. The result is disorder. It is the prelude to dictatorship, when ultimately one faction triumphs over all the others.

- ♦ **#5.**The Roman Empire was obsessed with law and order. Punishment of transgressors was extremely brutal. After Spartacus' slave revolt, 6,000 slaves (one fifth of the city's population) were crucified on the road to Rome. Their rotting bodies were left there for more than a year as an effective deterrent. No further slave revolts occurred thereafter. The final Jewish revolt was punished by the raising of Jerusalem to the ground and the great dispersion of the Jews. In the zealots' last stand at the Masada fortress, the overwhelmed rebels opted for collective suicide, to avoid facing Rome's retribution. Brutality and capital punishment aside, Roman law forms the basis of modern civil law. Having assimilated Greek philosophical concepts, Roman governance and administration is the basis of all the various forms of government throughout the ages-from the most democratic to the most totalitarian. Therefore, the tenets of the Roman Empire transcend time.**(Page121)**

IV.TYPES OF WARFARE

What types of warfare can you discern in the novel?

♦ Total war occurs when the warring nations mobilize the entire resources of the nation to wage war. It is self- destructive for both sides, particularly, if both sides are balanced in strength.

♦ A war of attrition is a long-term conflict waged by a weaker under-resourced enemy. The intention is to avoid open battle, and to conduct repeated small-scale surprise sabotage attacks. These are intended to wear down the superpower and to weaken its morale and resolve. It can also induce the superpower into awarding concessions in return for discontinuation of the debilitating hostilities.

♦ A war of retribution is a punitive, savage campaign intended to obliterate any opposition and to discourage opposition in the future. It is a vengeful disproportionate act by a superpower in response to the challenge of a weaker enemy. The SS Reich Protector of Bohemia, Reinhard Heydrich was assassinated in Prague. As a reprisal, the *Fuhrer* ordered that the two villages (with their inhabitants) falsely linked to the act of the resistance movement had to be eliminated. They were wiped out and they do not exist on the map anymore.

♦ Sedition is the means whereby unrest and disorder is engendered by dissemination of false provocative information that arouses discord. The perpetrators are known as agent provocateurs. They function like fire starters attempting to create a conflagration.

♦ Civil war occurs when two opposing factions in a country fight for their two conflicting ideals. These internecine wars are vicious and bleed the country of its lifeblood. Napoleon said that every European battle is in effect a European civil war. In a way, it is true because Europe started off as one huge country or empire. It subsequently split into nations each developing its own identity and culture. Most European wars have been fought over the positioning of borders between neighbours. Many borders are arbitrary and have changed repeatedly throughout history. The EU project is a way of Europe returning to its roots as one big country or empire through economic ties.

- A cold war occurs when two military superpowers vie for global dominance. They fear each other and avoid a direct confrontation which would be mutually self-destructive. However, they strive for that dominance by taking advantage of the instability in other countries. They do this by waging or sponsoring proxy wars in these volatile regions. As a result the world becomes polarised because different countries gravitate towards one or other superpower. The last cold war was between the U.S.A. and the U.S.S.R. The Middle East still remains fertile ground for the meddling power games of the superpowers.

How would you decide that a war is just?

- Either warring faction insists that they are in the right. It is not always easy to decide which faction's motive for war is just. It may be difficult to determine who is the aggressor and who is the victim. It makes a difference for the combatants, as they are dependent on foreign aid. The just side has a better chance of gaining sympathy and recruiting allies or vital resources. A set of guidelines was drafted by Saint Thomas Aquinas to decide if a war is just. However, even these can be misconstrued, as in the Second Gulf War.

V. JOURNALISM

Journalism is the reporting of the truth. It is known as the fourth estate and is an important check to the power of the rulers, especially in democratic countries. In dictatorships, it is suppressed.

- An investigative reporter functions like a detective and assesses the information to separate myth from fact. This type of journalist attempts to extricate the truth from the lie. It can be a dangerous occupation, when the power being investigated resorts to dirty or violent tactics to prevent the truth from being outed.

If you were an investigative journalist cat born just after Chief Miaow's death, how would you determine whether Miaow is saying the truth?

- You are confronted by two different versions of events .One is propagated by Miaow; the other is propagated by the majority but originates from the theories of George the fox.
- You need to interview key proponents of both versions to see which source is more credible. Since Miaow is dead, you have to interview his son, Captain Purr. For the other side, you have to interview George the fox.
- You have to corroborate their versions with other exponents on both sides of the spectrum to see if they are consistent.
- You would have to see whether the two proponents have any conflict of interest, what their motives are for sticking to those views and what they stand to gain or lose by propagating those views.
- Finally, you tally those versions with the facts as you see them now with your own eyes.

VI. MAN AS GUARDIAN OF THE ENVIRONMENT

How would you rate man's record as the master and guardian of the environment and wild life?

Very mixed, I am afraid.

On one side, you have the spiritual heirs of General Jack - the environmentalists and the lovers of nature. We have the whole works- animal hospitals, animal doctors, legislators against animal cruelty, the animal rights activists, the environmentalists and many other institutions.

On the other side, we have the destruction of the environment and the uncontrolled wanton extinction of wild life, through greed for money, for power or through indifference, downright cruelty or for sports, leisure and entertainment. The environment is sacrificed on the altar of capitalism. This is the utilitarian way of George the fox.

THE CHRONICLES OF OUR LAND

How would you like to give rein to the journalistic instinct within you, as Chief Miaow did? You can start now. Compose your views about Miaow's narrative. In that way, you become part of the story and you contribute to the Chronicles of Our Land. You become the spiritual heirs of Chief Miaow.

Send your reviews to Amazon and Goodreads.

Like Miaow, be brutally honest. Your reviews will be a tremendous help, if and when I write the third book of the Jack trilogy.

FROM THE AUTHOR

I

David Bush is a medical doctor specialized in haematology. He was born in Malta but left for the UK when he was in his early twenties. He returned to his first home in 2003 where he still practises hospital medicine. He is the co-founder of a support group for patients with blood cancers. Since he gave up his private practice, he has had more time to spend with the family. He enjoys reading, swimming, travelling and doing any type of DIY job. Most of all, though, he cherishes the time he spends with his young great-nephews Jack and Luke.

He has published many papers in international peer reviewed medical journals. He also writes analytical opinion articles for a satirical political blog.

This is the second book of the Jack trilogy in which his nephew becomes a protagonist in the plot. This trilogy-in-the-making was written for the protagonist's real life namesake nephew to be read by him at different ages. The author believes there is no better way to ignite a love of literature in a child other than with an in-house, self-published work. This arduous literary DIY undertaking was a labour of love from beginning to end.

II

This short fable is deeply textured and multi-layered with a variety of intertwining themes.

Superficially, the novel is a fantasy adventure of humanized animals interacting with a boy. The tale provides an original and entertaining alternative historical take on the evolution of nature and wild life.

Just below the surface, it becomes obvious that this is a parody on politics and military history in the tradition of "Animal Farm." It is intended to educate and stimulate young readers' interest in politics and history.

At a third, deeper and more personal level, it is a story of redemptive character development. The main character, Miaow embarks on a journey of self-discovery. The external conflict reflects the inner psychological conflict of the main character. It is a struggle between flesh and spirit narrated in Francois Mauriac's naturalistic style.

At a fourth and even deeper level, the novel is allegorical in the vein of "The Chronicles of Narnia". The novel becomes a retelling of the transcendent Parable of the Sower. General Jack is the Christ-like figure who is the bearer of the Good News. In essence, the story is a parable of the scriptural parable.

On another even deeper spiritual, but personal level, it is a fictional allegory of the relationship between Saint John the Evangelist (represented by Miaow) and Jesus. The filial relationship between Miaow and Jackat is a fictional reconstruction of the ties between the Evangelist Apostle and Polycarp, the first Father of the early Christian Church.

The author uses the literary techniques of three giants of modern literature - George Orwell, Francois Mauriac and C.S. Lewis - to create a deceptively simple saga. In no way can the text of the book ever match the literary style and prose of these three literary masters, all Nobel Prize laureates. The voice of the book is raw, cynical but sincere reflecting the restlessness of the narrator who bares his tortured soul.

The early Christian community was defenceless under the ruthlessly almighty Roman regime that tolerated no challenge to its hegemony. The discussion of Jesus' teachings was considered to be a seditious act against the authority of the emperor. It was punished by a death as violent and sadistic as possible. They were even fed to the lions in the arena.

Polycarp was one of the three Apostolic Church Fathers, so named because they lived during the generation of the Apostles and they were their direct disciples. Polycarp was the most well-connected and prestigious having been mentored and ordained by the Apostle John at a young age. Because of his intimate relation to the Evangelist, he was the most influential elder of the early church. Polycarp lived in a precarious age after the death of the Apostles, when myriad interpretations of Jesus' life were being peddled. Some were genuine, many others were outright false or distortions of the truth. One of his roles was to authenticate the orthodox versions or teachings by virtue of his well known personal connection to John. This book is an ode to the Church Fathers. They sacrificed their lives under brutally, hostile imperial Roman rule to preserve the inspired Word uncorrupted for eternity. The Christian world owes them a great debt. The author's little book honours the greatest book ever written, and the indomitable little people who risked all to hand it down to us in its pure, untainted form.

III

John and Polycarp lived unusually long lives. John died of natural causes at the age of ninety-four in AD100.The tireless Polycarp was martyred at the age of eighty-six in AD155, but not before mentoring the boy who would then become St. Irenaeus of Lyons, the great ante-Nicene Church Father.

This story is an allegorical fable that narrates the history of salvation in an imaginary animal world before time. It documents the advent of the boy messiah and the ensuing clash between the two leaders of the seen and unseen worlds. The drama prefigures the history of the salvation of mankind in the first century that rages on in perpetuity (in a mystical sense).

The novel allegorizes the political milieu in the first hundred years of Christianity. There were five political groups in Palestine at the time but one group ruled them all.

1.The Roman imperial dictatorship that provided harsh law and order. They made the only exception in their empire and delegated limited regional government to the Israelites.

2.The Pharisees were the largest political faction, precursors of the socialist movement. They oversaw a rudimentary socialist welfare state.

3.The Sadducees were the upper class wealthy landowner class. They were organized into a nationalist conservative group that colluded with the Roman emperor to wrest concessions for themselves.

These two political groups were bitter rivals who convened regularly in the Jewish assembly where they debated and voted on various policies. Although the two parties had the preservation of Jewish identity at heart, they could agree on little else. The larger Pharisee party was fanatical and abused of theology to maintain their hold on the people. The Sadducees gave only nominal attention to the Jewish faith and were mostly capitalist. Both co-governing parties were money-minded, power hungry and self-serving.

4.The libertine Herodians were a small liberal party on relatively good terms with their colonial masters, to whom they pandered.
5.The Maccabean zealots were the radical party that advocated armed struggle against their overlords. Their revolt was to instigate the destruction of Jerusalem and the great dispersion of the Jews.

There were two other disenfranchised, powerless groups with no political aspirations:

1.The downtrodden Samaritans who were ostracized because they were of mixed race. They were the offspring of Jews who had assimilated with foreign immigrants.
2.The innocuous and pacifist Essenes (can anything good come out of Nazareth? John 1:46), out of which Christianity was to take root and eventually take over the world.

The political landscape in Palestine of that time is a microcosm of government throughout the ages up to modern times.

The two brothers, John and James were the sons of Zebedee and of Mary Salome, the sister of the Blessed Virgin. They were known as the sons of thunder although John was docile, unlike his more forceful brother. At the time of Jesus' arrest, both John and James fled for their lives. But John reappeared with his own mother at Calvary. Both risked their lives when standing bravely by both Jesus' and the Blessed Virgin's side during the Passion. What made the fearful apostle stand by the Blessed Virgin in such a hostile, intimidating scenario? Was it the influence of his fearless and loyal mother? We do not know and it is beside the point. But behind every great man, there has to be a formidable woman.

The character of Sabine is a tribute to John's mother, Mary Salome. She had been inopportune enough to pressure Jesus into allowing her two sons (to the consternation of the other disciples) to have the privilege of "sitting one at your right and the other at your left in your kingdom." (Matthew 20:21) This impertinent petition was gently brushed aside. She was the first witness of the empty tomb together with the two other Marys. She headed this group determined to perform the impossible task of anointing a lifeless person. Impossible, because she was aware that three women could not roll away the stone (weighing about 2000 kg or just over two tons) that sealed the tomb. But still they went, such was their devotion. On arrival at the empty tomb, they were favoured by an angelic visitation announcing the Resurrection. Mary Magdalene was not convinced and she lingered by the tomb, while Mary Salome, together with her sister-in-law Mary Cleopas, returned to inform the cowering fugitive apostles who did not believe the good news.

In this novel, Sabine matures into a dynamic, devoted and fearless maternal figure for doubting Miaow and his family, giving them the sense of direction and drive they so sorely needed.

Scratchy's character resembles that of James who was the first apostle to be executed for his faith in AD 44. He travelled far and wide, reaching the Western fringes of the Roman Empire. He is the patron saint of Spain and his remains rest in Santiago de Compostela which is a popular pilgrimage for the faithful who retrace the "Way of Saint James". He is the only apostle to be called "the Great".

Twinkle is a fictional adumbration of Mary Magdalene. A sensual, naïve but endearing character who would have easily lost her way if it were not for the protection provided by Miaow and Sabine. Left to her own means, the wealthy Mary Magdalene was to fall into bad company, but under the appropriate guidance, she was to flourish and achieve immortality, becoming a revered figure in Christianity.

OTHER BOOKS BY THE AUTHOR

The Joyous Adventures of Whizzojack

A five year old boy considers himself a superhero and uses his "superpowers" to protect the people of Jacktown from a host of colourful supervillains, or does he make matters worse?

Spiderman juggles with Aesop in this 21st century Parable of the Talents.

This is the first book of the Jack trilogy. It is an illustrated chapter book intended for children between 5 and 8 years.

It is available from Amazon in both paperback and e-book formats.

CLOSING CREDITS

The graphic illustrators of Shutterstock are hereby credited for the images used in the book in order of appearance. Each illustrator's entire portfolio can be accessed through Shutterstock.

Vidoslava, ArtMari, Andrija Markovic, Cosmo Vector, BigAlis Saloo, Robert Adrian Hillman.
Chapter 1. Part I: Theo Malings, Nemanja Cosovic, Tonkaa, Ales Krivec, Paul Looyen, Vepeya. **Part II:** Dean Zangirolami, Seita, **Part III:** Janista.
Part IV: Les Perysty, Sundora14, OzZon, Shaineast, Zhenyakot,   Robin Nieuwenkamp.
Part V: Shaineast.
 PartVI: Julia_fdt.
 Alexokokok,Sahan2u.
Part VII: Panda Vector, Arcady.
Chapter 2. Part I: Kuttelva_Serova
Stuchelova. **Part II:** Eladora, Nadzeya
Shanchuk, Spes Vini,
Chipmunk131, Cattallina, TcoiE. **Part III**: James Weston,

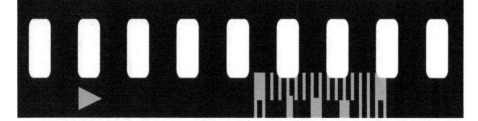

Chapter13. Part I: Hollygraphic.
Part II: Lightly Stranded
Happiness-income, Nikola M, Gaikova, Sylvie Corriveau,
Janna Mudrak
Chapter 14. Part I: Irina Bushveva, **Part II**: Vzhyshnevska
 Nataliia, Angela Jones, Vetochka, Wong Salam,
Wan Ching Chen.
Part III: Lizzillustrations, Naddya, Nenad Leskov, Rudall30.
Sewonboy
Appendix: Flat_Enot,
S. Hanusch,
Erik Steinebach,
TotemArt,VikiVector,Tatiana Popova.

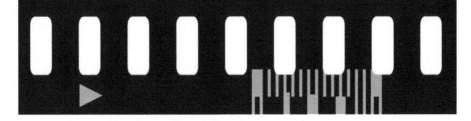

Made in the USA
Monee, IL
30 January 2021